MW01075968

THE APOSTLE CONSPIRACY

VATICAN SECRET ARCHIVE THRILLERS
BOOK NINE

GARY MCAVOY

LITERATI
EDITIONS.

Copyright © 2024 by Gary McAvoy

All rights reserved. No part of this publication may be reproduced, distributed, or transmitted in any form or by any means, including photocopying, recording, or other electronic or mechanical methods, without the prior written permission of the publisher, except in the case of brief quotations embodied in critical reviews and certain other noncommercial uses permitted under current copyright law. For permission requests, write to the publisher using the email or postal address below.

Hardcover ISBN: 978-1-954123-53-3
Paperback ISBN: 978-1-954123-52-6
eBook ISBN: 978-1-954123-51-9

Library of Congress Control Number: 2024923590

Published by:
Literati Editions
PO Box 5987
Bremerton WA 98312
Email: info@LiteratiEditions.com
Visit the author's website: www.GaryMcAvoy.com

This is a work of fiction. Names, characters, businesses, places, long-standing institutions, agencies, public offices, events, locales, and incidents are either the products of the author's imagination or have been used in a fictitious manner. Apart from historical references, any resemblance to actual persons, living or dead, or actual events is purely coincidental.

All trademarks are the property of their respective owners. Neither Gary McAvoy nor Literati Editions is associated with any product or vendor mentioned in this book.

This book contains original and copyrighted material that is not intended to be used for the purpose of training Artificial Intelligence (AI) systems. The author and publisher of this book prohibit the use of any part of this book for AI training, machine learning, or any other similar purpose without prior written permission.

The author and publisher do not endorse or authorize the use of this book for AI training, and shall not be liable for any damages arising from such unauthorized use. Any unauthorized use of this book for AI training is strictly prohibited and may violate applicable laws and regulations.

The author and publisher reserve all rights, including but not limited to, the right to seek damages and injunctive relief, against any person or entity that uses this book for AI training without prior written permission.

If you wish to use any part of this book for AI training, please contact the author and publisher to obtain written permission.

BOOKS BY GARY MCAVOY

FICTION

The Apostle Conspiracy

The Celestial Guardian

The Confessions of Pope Joan

The Galileo Gambit

The Jerusalem Scrolls

The Avignon Affair

The Petrus Prophecy

The Opus Dictum

The Vivaldi Cipher

The Magdalene Veil

The Magdalene Reliquary

The Magdalene Deception

NONFICTION

And Every Word Is True

PROLOGUE

FIRST CENTURY – ROME

The year was AD 64, and Rome, the heart of an empire that stretched across the known world, was cloaked in a thick blanket of smoke and ashes. A great fire had raged through the Eternal City for seven days and seven nights, leaving a significant part of it in ruins. The once vibrant streets and bustling marketplaces lay smoldering, their echoes silenced by the calamity.

Emperor Nero, from the golden balcony of his sprawling palace, watched over his capital with a gaze that flickered between dismay and a dark, unspoken euphoria. Rumors swirled mercilessly like the smoke that rose from the city—rumors that Nero himself had set the city ablaze to make room for his grandiose architectural fantasies. But in the politically charged atmosphere of Rome, where the truth was often sacrificed at the altar of convenience, a scapegoat was needed to quell the public outcry. And Nero had found his.

Within days of the fire's subsidence, the Christians, a small but growing sect despised for their disdain of Roman deities, were rounded up. Among them was an old man, a simple fisherman, robust in spirit but now frail in body, known among his brethren as Simon. Rumor had it that he was a close confidante of the crucified Nazarene called Jesus, whom many hailed as the Messiah, and who had given Simon the Aramaic name "Cephas," translated as Peter—the rock upon whom His Church would be built.

Under escort by the Praetorian Guard, Peter was dragged through streets where he had walked freely just weeks before, now lined with citizens who cast stones and slurs with equal fervor. They reached the Circus of Nero, a vast, open space used for public entertainments that now served as the stage for a grim spectacle.

The charges against him were as absurd as they were severe—arson, treason against the divine majesty of Rome, and the corruption of Roman morals with foreign superstitions. Adorned in a robe as purple as the bruises on Peter's aged body, Nero presided over the farcical trial. The evidence was scant, testimonies coerced, and the verdict foregone.

As the sentence was declared, the crowd erupted in a mixture of cheers and jeers. Peter was to be crucified, an execution method reserved for the lowest of criminals, a symbol of extreme humiliation and excruciating pain. Yet, in his final moments of judgment, Peter requested a last, bizarre act of mercy—that he be crucified upside down, as he deemed himself unworthy to die in the same manner as his Lord.

His request granted with a scoff, Peter was led to his gruesome fate. As the cross was raised, the upside-down figure of the old man became a poignant symbol against the backdrop of the smoldering city. His eyes, filled with an otherworldly peace, gazed skyward, fixated on a realm beyond the smoke and flames.

As Peter breathed his last, his followers, hidden within the shadows, whispered prayers and wept silently. They knew this was not the end of his story. In the darkness of that day, the seeds of a legacy were sown, one that would grow to outlive the empire that sought to crush it—a legacy of faith, resilience, and the indomitable spirit of a man known to history as St. Peter, Prince of the Apostles and, by tradition, the first Pope of the Roman Catholic Church.

As THE DAWN of the tenth century painted the Roman skyline with hues of gold and crimson, the ancient city bore the scars of time but none so revered as the Basilica of St. Peter. Constructed under the decree of Emperor Constantine in AD 324, the mammoth structure had been erected atop the site believed to cradle the remains of St. Peter, marking a pivotal shift in the religious landscape of the Roman Empire from pagan roots to a bastion of Christianity.

Over the centuries, the basilica had become a beacon

for pilgrims from across Christendom, drawn not only to its sacred aura but to the promise of being near the earthly remains of the Apostle Peter. Yet, as devout as the visits were, the exact location of Peter's tomb beneath the sprawling church had grown obscure, cloaked in layers of marble and mystery and the shifting sands of theology and politics.

It was not until a series of unforeseen events in the early 900s that the ancient whispers about the apostle's bones would stir the soil once more. The basilica, aged and weary from bearing the weight of centuries, required extensive renovations to preserve its grandeur and sacredness. It was during this period of restoration, under the watchful guidance of Pope John X, that a remarkable discovery was made.

Tasked with reinforcing the foundations of the altar, a group of workers, under the dim glow of torchlight, unearthed a hidden subterranean chamber directly beneath the towering Baldacchino bronze canopy that covered the high altar of the basilica. The air was thick with dust and sanctity as the overseer, a pious man named Gregorio, was called over by the workers to peer into the forgotten crypt. Inside, amid the relics of time and fragments of pottery, lay a simple stone sarcophagus, its lid adorned with faint inscriptions and primitive Christian symbols, graffiti that was unmistakably early in origin. The chamber proved to lead to secret tunnels branching out and leading to other parts of the Vatican.

The discovery sent ripples through the ecclesiastical hierarchy. Scholars and clerics were summoned, and careful examination began. The inscriptions, though worn, bore the telling marks of reverence: a Christian cross, figures of heavenly keys, and the words "*Petros eni.*" In Ancient Greek, ENI was often used as a contraction of the verb ENEOTI, meaning "is within." The consensus took this to mean, "Peter is buried here." Moreover, the positioning of the sarcophagus, directly below the altar of the old basilica, aligned too perfectly with the records of Constantine's builders for it to be a mere coincidence.

With a mixture of reverence and trepidation, the sarcophagus was opened. Inside, the bones were modest, those of a sturdy, elderly man, consistent with historical accounts of Peter's martyrdom. As word of the discovery spread, the basilica swelled with crowds hungry for a glimpse of the connection to the foundation of their faith.

In AD 914, Pope John X, recognizing the significance of the find, ordered the immediate resanctification of the tomb. A series of solemn ceremonies were held, attended by dignitaries and common folk alike, each eager to reaffirm their faith through the tangible remnants of their sainted apostle. The bones of Peter were carefully reentombed in a newly constructed shrine under the altar, this time with full honors and the eyes of the Christian world watching.

The rediscovery of St. Peter's bones not only rejuvenated the spiritual life of Rome but also reasserted the papacy's authority, which had waned under political pressures from both within and outside the Church. It was a moment of unity and revival, a reaffirmation of a centuries-old legacy that continued to shape the contours of Christian doctrine and devotion.

Thus, as the tenth century progressed, St. Peter's Basilica stood not only as a monument to the Christianization of the Roman Empire but as a living testament to the enduring power of faith and the eternal watch of its founding shepherd over the flock he left behind.

CHAPTER
ONE

PRESENT DAY

The skies over Seattle were a tapestry of brooding clouds, a fitting backdrop to the sprawling estate of Elliot Voss situated in Hunts Point, an upscale enclave on the secluded outskirts of the city. The grounds were meticulously manicured, bordered by dense woods that whispered secrets with the wind. At the heart of this domain stood Voss Technologies' headquarters, a masterpiece of modern architecture, its glass façade reflecting the turbulent skies of the Pacific Northwest.

Beneath this citadel of innovation, far from the prying eyes of the world, lay Elliot Voss's most guarded possession—a state-of-the-art museum vault. This was no ordinary repository of valuables or corporate secrets; it housed a collection that would make the most seasoned curator pale—religious artifacts gathered from the darkest corners of history, each with a story soaked in mystic lore.

Elliot Voss stood at the entrance to this underground sanctuary, his silhouette a sharp contrast against the biometrically sealed door that responded only to his presence. With a slight nod, he initiated the opening sequence, and the door slid away with a hiss, revealing the sanctum that fed his obsession and fueled his ambitions.

Inside, the vault was a cathedral of the arcane and the profound. Climate-controlled glass cases lined the walls, each illuminated with soft, reverential lighting that cast an ethereal glow on their contents. Here lay shards of pottery rumored to be from the very chalice of the Last Supper; there, the tattered remnants of a robe said to have belonged to Joan of Arc; and in a particularly unassuming case, a fragment of wood believed to be from the True Cross.

Voss walked among these relics with the air of a zealot, his eyes reflecting a fire that burned with an unquenchable curiosity and desire. His footsteps echoed in the vault as he approached a central console, where screens displayed data streams that monitored every aspect of the room, from humidity to security.

At this console he paused, his gaze fixating on a particular case that held his latest acquisition—a dusty, age-worn scroll purported to contain lost Gnostic gospels. It was a testament to his reach and resources, having been secured through shadowy channels that intertwined with the illicit and the clandestine.

His gloved hand reached with reverence toward the

scroll, yet he did not touch it, for he knew the fragility of history and the cataclysmic loss it would be should this scroll crumble under his fingers. The scroll had been in his possession for days now and each day he returned, awaiting his technology's translation to reveal what secrets the cryptic images might hold for him alone.

A soft beep from the console drew his attention back. His breath held, his fingers danced gracefully over the keys of the console as he called up the now deciphered translation of the scroll. The text was cryptic and labyrinthine, a pattern of allegories and metaphors that would have left any ordinary mind confounded.

But Elliot Voss was no ordinary man. After a careful few minutes, the message came clear. The translation spoke of St. Peter's bones being imbued with divine power. It hinted at secrets hidden within their marrow—keys to unlocking human regeneration and longevity. The potential to extract these energies and fuse them with Voss's advanced technology sparked possibilities too tantalizing to ignore. The ability to manipulate biological life at its core was within his grasp, potentially offering him immortality and, with that, possibly even control over human will.

A shadow twisted across his face—a mix of hunger and fear as he pondered this power. He had always believed in destiny, in predestination. The thought of transcending human limits, of attaining the immortality of godhood, brought forth an intoxicating thrill where every beat of his heart felt like the loud footsteps of destiny approaching.

With this awe-inspiring revelation sending currents

of excitement rushing through his veins, he sank into the chair, his gaze never leaving the cryptic text on the screen. The potential was beyond astronomical; the profound implications of this discovery surpassed any tangible comprehension. It was the holy grail of humanity, a leap toward immortality wrapped in age-old scriptures.

Heaving a sigh as if to release the breath he didn't realize he had been holding, Voss stood and turned, surveying the room full of treasures. His dark eyes flitted from one artifact to another, each holding secrets that could shatter the foundation of knowledge humanity had built over thousands of years. All his efforts collecting these had led to this—the one artifact that held the key to his destiny. With that key, he had only to retrieve one more artifact to fulfill that destiny. None other of his "finds" held power as potent as the one treasure he coveted now more than any other—the bones of the Apostle St. Peter, currently secured in the Vatican.

He moved away from the console and began to pace in front of the scroll, his mind a whirlwind of thoughts. Though he was alone within the vault, there was a sense that he was being watched, that every decision he made within this hallowed ground was subject to unseen judgment. He cast a glance toward the remnants of St. Joan's robe, remembering the tales of her visions and divine guidance. Would she condemn this pursuit of godhood or recognize it as a holy mission bestowed upon him?

Returning to the console, Voss began accessing

another file, this one pertaining to his ongoing Voss Laboratory biological research. Charts and graphs filled the screen as he studied the results carefully. His team was on the brink of breakthroughs; their experiments had shown promise in genetically manipulating cells for regrowth and enhanced performance.

The implications were clear: if they could harness the power within St. Peter's bones and integrate that with their current research, they could potentially rewrite humanity's DNA. Such immense power would bring about a new era—an era where death was not an end but an unnecessary pause, where life could be extended indefinitely.

The glorious dream of immortality, he knew, had a precipitous flip side. The whispers of caution from history's greatest tragedies echoed in his mind, reminding him of Icarus, who flew too close to the sun, or Pandora's box, which, once opened, unleashed more than what was bargained for.

Voss fell into deep thought, his gaze again drawn to each artifact in turn—each one a testament to faith, conviction, and sacrifice, each one bearing witness to history's tendency to repeat itself in cycles of triumph and devastation. Could his pursuit of immortality and control incite another cycle? Could it be that this vault of relics served not just as a collection of history's mystical remnants but also as cautionary tales?

With every tick reverberating through the silent vault, Voss felt closer to making a decision that would irrevocably alter the course of human evolution. The allure of immortality gnawed at him, each artifact in his collection jeering and cheering in equal measure. A multitude of possible futures played out in his mind like a reel of film, each one more dramatic and tantalizing than the last.

His eyes lingered on the scroll once more. It was not just an artifact; it was a map to a forbidden treasure filled with hidden depths and unexplored possibilities. And Voss, with his relentless ambition, unquenchable curiosity, and virtually unlimited resources was ready to navigate its labyrinthine paths, regardless of where they may lead.

"Elliot, the system diagnostics are complete. All artifacts are stable," chimed a voice from the console, the AI assistant that managed the operations of the vault.

"Thank you, Ada," Voss replied, his voice steady but tinged with an underlying anticipation. "Prepare the analysis module. It's time we unlocked further secrets."

As the AI hummed in compliance, Voss turned his attention back to the collection. Each piece was a node in a network of power he was meticulously wiring—a power not of this world but of a realm that danced on the edge of the divine and the eternal. His belief was unshakeable: within these relics lay the keys to transcendent human capabilities, to mastering not just the mortal coil but also the essence of fate itself.

His phone buzzed discreetly, a reminder of the dual life he led. On the surface, he was the brash young CEO of a tech giant, a visionary pushing the boundaries of AI and biotech. But here, underground, he was a seeker of truths hidden since the dawn of recorded time. Not wishing to be disturbed, he let the call go to Ada, who would route it accordingly.

Voss stood in silence for several long moments, lost in contemplation. Then, with a solemn nod to himself, he engaged the locking mechanisms on the console and turned to leave the vault. His Gulfstream G700 was being prepared for a flight to Italy, leaving within the hour, so getting to Boeing Field was the priority.

As he emerged from the vault, Voss saw the storm that had been brewing in the Seattle skies break with a brilliant flash of lightning followed by a deafening clap of thunder, as if in answer to his philosophical thoughts. A prophetic reckoning of the cataclysm that might befall should Elliot Voss unlock the secrets of life and death. He knew his pursuit for immortality had only just begun; a quest that could ultimately cost humanity more than it could possibly comprehend. For what is man but mortal? And what does he become when he breaks those shackles?

The journey toward immortality was fraught with dangers, not only for Voss but also for a world that was blissfully unaware of the tempest gathering force beneath its feet.

CHAPTER

TWO

The modernist sweep of the Paul VI Audience Hall stood in stark contrast to the ancient, intricate architecture of St. Peter's Basilica nearby. Inside, the vast hall was shaped like a ship's hull, a symbolic ark nestled in the heart of the Vatican. Late afternoon sunlight poured through the elongated stained-glass windows, casting angular patches of light across the auditorium and its attendees.

The interior, though stark, was filled with an air of anticipation. The seats, arranged in gently curving rows, were mostly filled with an eclectic mix of clergy, scholars, journalists, and curious visitors. At the front, a large stage was set with a single podium, behind which a huge digital screen displayed a rotating selection of ancient documents and texts.

Father Michael Dominic, Prefect of the Vatican Apostolic Archives, stood at the podium, a figure of calm and authority. Speaking in Italian, his voice resonated clearly through the modern sound system, reaching every corner of the hall.

"And so, ladies and gentlemen, as we advance further into the digital era, the task of preserving our historical documents becomes both more feasible and more imperative. We have the technology to prevent the physical decay of these priceless texts, but we must also guard against the digital decay and potential manipulation of these records. It is our responsibility, our duty, to maintain the integrity of our history."

Applause filled the room as Father Michael gestured toward a slide of a digitally restored medieval manuscript.

As the applause subsided, the priest continued, "The process is intricate and delicate. Every page, every word is scanned, analyzed, and digitally reconstructed. Yet the work is not tedious, but a timeless communion with our forebears."

He gestured toward the massive screen which now showed a vividly colorful fresco from an ancient chapel in Sicily. "Look at the beauty we can preserve," he said, his voice swelling with reverence. "These are not just books or paintings, but testaments to our faith and our history."

A murmur of approval echoed through the hall as the fresco disappeared to be replaced by a medieval Bible's painstakingly illuminated page. The audience watched in awe as digital enhancement brought forth details that time had cruelly caused to fade away.

Father Michael paused, letting the silent beauty of the image fill the room. Then he spoke again, softer now.

"But this is not just about preservation," he said, "it's about accessibility." His hand swept over the audience as though inviting them in. "These treasures should be seen and studied by all who seek knowledge and understanding."

He nodded toward a side door and two assistants wheeled in a cart bearing an ancient volume bound in worn leather. The murmurs grew louder as people recognized it as one of the most precious treasures of the Vatican Library—the *Codex Vaticanus*.

"We are proud to announce," Michael said with a glint of excitement in his eyes, "that this priceless gem has been our latest project." He had to raise his voice to be heard over the gasps and excited chatter now filling the hall.

As he revealed a digital rendering of one of its beautifully illustrated pages on the screen behind him, spontaneous applause erupted once again. It was clear that under Father Michael Dominic's guidance, history was being delicately cradled into the future with a respect for the past that left everyone present in complete awe.

"I will now take any questions you may have."

From the second row, an attractive young woman with chestnut-brown hair raised her hand. A microphone was passed to her by one of the ushers, and she stood, commanding yet respectful.

"Father Dominic, Hana Sinclair from *Le Monde*. You spoke eloquently about the risks and rewards of digital preservation. However, with the increasing sophistication of digital manipulation, how can we ensure that future generations receive a true and unaltered account of history? Isn't there a danger that by digitizing these documents, we could be paving the way for unintended repercussions?"

The audience murmured, intrigued by the question as she remained standing for the answer. Michael met her gaze, a slight knowing smile crossing his face as he nodded to his friend in appreciation.

"Ms. Sinclair, that is indeed an astute observation and highlights one of the formidable challenges we face in the realm of digital preservation. To address these concerns, the Vatican is not merely adapting but innovating with multiple layers of security protocols. Among these, we are pioneering the use of blockchain technology to forge an immutable ledger of our historical documents."

He paused momentarily, allowing the audience to absorb the implications of using such advanced technology in the preservation of ancient texts.

"This ledger is not just a record; it is a testament to our commitment to maintain the authenticity of documents that have shaped the very foundation of our civilization. Each document encoded into this blockchain is time-stamped, its integrity cryptographically secured, making it virtually tamper-proof. But while technology offers a shield against many threats, it introduces new ethical dilemmas."

Michael's tone became introspective, reflecting the complexity of the issue.

"Your question, Ms. Sinclair, touches upon a deeper, more profound ethical dimension: how do we preserve the sanctity of truth itself in this digital frontier? This is not just a technical challenge but a moral imperative. The truth is the bedrock of our history, our culture, and our faith. As we digitize these texts, we must ask ourselves: are we merely keepers of knowledge, or are we guardians of truth?"

He looked around the hall, engaging directly with the audience members who nodded in agreement, drawn in by the significance of his words.

"In this endeavor, the role of continuous collaboration with the media, academic scholars, and technology experts becomes not just beneficial but essential. Together, we must forge a new path forward— one that respects the legacy of the past while embracing the possibilities of the future. We must build partnerships that reinforce our commitment to transparency and ethical stewardship."

Gesturing emphatically, he continued with a call to action.

"We, together with you—journalists, historians, technologists, and scholars—must remain vigilant. We must be the guardians of our history, ensuring that as we step into the future, we do not lose sight of the authenticity and integrity of our past. It is a monumental task, yet it is one we must undertake with dedication and integrity. Let us commit to this guardianship, to maintaining the sanctity of our collective history. For in preserving our past accurately and ethically, we safeguard the future's ability to understand its roots and learn from them."

As Michael concluded, a resonant wave of applause

erupted, reflecting the collective recognition of the challenges and the crucial role of collaborative vigilance in addressing them. His words not only spoke to the technical aspects of digital preservation but also called for an ethical consensus on maintaining the fidelity of historical narratives in the digital age.

Hana nodded, her expression thoughtful as she thanked the priest and took her seat.

Another member of the audience, a stout man in his sixties, raised his hand. The microphone was brought to him as the man stood and addressed Michael.

"Father Dominic, thank you for your enlightening presentation. My question concerns the accessibility of these digitally preserved documents. While securing these documents against manipulation is paramount, how does the Vatican plan to balance this with public access? Is there a strategy to ensure that these treasures of history are not just safely preserved but also made available to researchers and the public globally without compromising their integrity?"

Michael listened intently to the question, nodding slightly as he formulated his response.

"An excellent question, and indeed, it touches upon one of the most crucial aspects of our digital archiving initiatives. The Vatican holds documents that are not only religiously significant but also of immense historical value to scholars, researchers, and the general public worldwide."

He gestured toward the screen behind him, which shifted to display a colorful graph of digital access statistics.

"As we endeavor to protect these documents from digital tampering and decay, we are equally committed to making them accessible. Our strategy encompasses several key elements: First, we are developing a tiered access system. This system ensures that the most sensitive documents are protected through restricted access, while still providing ample material available more broadly. For example, preliminary documents, certain translations, and non-sensitive writings are accessible online to the public and researchers without compromising the originals' sanctity or security."

He shifted slightly, now engaging directly with the audience at large.

"Secondly, we are collaborating with global institutions to facilitate remote access. By partnering with universities and libraries worldwide, we can provide terminals through which authenticated users can access high-quality digital facsimiles of our archives. This approach not only broadens accessibility but also ensures that the documents are used within a controlled environment, minimizing the risk of misuse.

"Furthermore, we are investing in cutting-edge technology to create detailed digital replicas of each document. This includes high-resolution imaging and, in some cases, 3D modeling of seals and inscriptions. This technology not only aids in preservation but enhances the user experience, allowing for an interaction with the text that is as close to the real thing as possible without ever touching the original.

"Lastly, we are continuously exploring advancements in encryption and blockchain to ensure that these digital replicas, while accessible, remain unalterable once they are created. It is a delicate balance, indeed, but one we approach with the utmost care and respect for both the documents themselves and the global community that seeks to learn from them."

"Thank you, Father. I'm sure we all appreciate your thoughtful remarks on the topic. I certainly do."

As the audience applauded, Michael checked his watch. "Are there any more questions?"

The hall was silent for a moment as heads turned to see if any other hands rose, when a striking, well-groomed man looking to be in his thirties, dressed all in black including a narrow black tie, quietly stood and hailed the usher with his raised hand. The microphone was brought to him, and as he held it, looking directly at Michael for a few silent moments, he slowly lifted it to his mouth.

"Father Dominic," he began in English, the deep resonance of his commanding voice causing the amplified speakers to rumble and flutter, "I understand the Vatican has planned a special celebration honoring the 1100th anniversary of the resanctification of St. Peter's bones in a few weeks. While I appreciate your dedication to preserving such an invaluable part of Christian heritage, given the extreme age and the fragility of these relics, isn't it potentially hazardous to move and display them, especially considering the throngs of visitors expected for such an event?" His eyes, sharp and unyielding, fixed on the priest, as if searching for any hint of uncertainty.

Michael, maintaining a composed demeanor,

responded thoughtfully, "Well, though it is rather off topic for this presentation, that is an excellent question and a valid concern. I assure you, the Vatican takes the utmost care with all relics, particularly those as sacred as the bones of St. Peter. For that occasion, the relics will be encased in a specially designed, climate-controlled, bulletproof glass container. Moreover, the display will be brief and monitored at all times by our top security personnel to ensure their protection from any damage or other risks."

The questioner nodded slightly, seemingly satisfied with the answer but still intense in his scrutiny. "Thank you, Father," said the man, his voice softening a fraction. "It is reassuring to hear of the extensive measures being taken to protect such a pivotal piece of history." Handing back the microphone, he slowly took his seat.

The audience murmured amongst themselves, impressed with the thoughtful exchange and the precautions described by the priest. Meanwhile, Michael couldn't shake off a subtle intuition that the questioner, with his meticulously chosen words and piercing gaze, had more than a mere passing interest in the relics. He made a mental note to inquire about the identity of the man in black, his instincts telling him that there might be more to his question than simple curiosity. Too, there was something vaguely familiar about him, though he couldn't place it at the moment.

Michael again glanced at his watch.

"It appears I've gone well over the prescribed time for our presentation, but I do hope you've gained something in the process. I want to thank you for being such a fine audience." There was more applause as people began standing and making their way toward exits marked by the posting of a Swiss Guard at each door.

As Michael gathered his materials on the podium, Hana made her way up the broad steps of the stage. Before speaking, she reached up and switched off the microphone.

"Nicely done, Michael," she said. "Even I learned things I had no idea were involved in your work."

"I feel like I just touched on the surface of things, to be honest, but the time seems to have flown by. You up for an early dinner?"

"I was hoping you'd ask. I'm starving." Turning around to watch the audience leave, Hana saw her cousin Karl Dengler and his partner Lukas Bischoff coming up an aisle toward the stage, dressed in the colorful Renaissance uniforms of the Pontifical Swiss Guard, their traditional halberds in hand. Reaching the podium, Karl smiled broadly as he greeted them.

"Nice job, Michael. You really know your stuff. You should do this more often."

"Thanks, Karl, but I'd prefer keeping these presentations to a minimum. The prep is just too time-consuming. Hey, are you and Lukas free to join us for dinner? We're heading over to Burrata Bistro now."

Looking up at Lukas, Karl's face betrayed his disappointment. "We'd love to, but we've got another hour left on our shift, and it does take time to get out of these uniforms. Rain check?"

"You bet. Any time," the priest said.

Looking out over the departing crowd, he happened to see the man in black standing alone toward the rear of the hall, just staring back at Michael. Once their eyes met, the man suddenly broke the gaze, slowly turned, and walked out the exit.

THREE

B aron Armand de Saint-Clair, the esteemed chairman of Banque Suisse de Saint-Clair, was seated at an ornate desk in the opulent study of his suite at the Rome Cavalieri Waldorf Astoria, located just north of the sacred precincts of the Vatican. The room was filled with the rich aroma of freshly brewed coffee, thanks to Armand's diligent assistant, Frederic, who meticulously tended to his master's needs. Across from Armand sat Elliot Voss, the dynamic and successful American entrepreneur, who also happened to be a valued member of Armand's bank's board of directors.

As Frederic quietly refilled their cups with steaming hot coffee, Voss leaned forward, his eyes reflecting a keen interest as he spoke. "Armand," he began, his voice carrying a tone of earnestness, "as you are well aware, I'm deeply invested in the collection of some of the finest manuscripts and artifacts from the ancient world. I firmly believe that we have a solemn duty as guardians of history to ensure that these treasures are preserved for the enlightenment of future generations."

He paused for a moment, letting his words sink in before continuing. "That's why I'd like to extend my personal resources to assist the Vatican in their ongoing efforts to preserve, protect, and further research the invaluable items housed within the Secret Archives. Given your unique connection with the Prefect of the Archives, I was hoping you might facilitate an introduction."

The baron, who was usually composed and unflappable, found himself hesitating as he mentally processed Voss's request. This was a moment requiring diplomatic finesse and utmost prudence, and Armand knew he had to tread carefully. Voss was a formidable presence on Armand's board for the bank; all too often, his voice held more influence, even if not more authority, than the other members' voices. Yet Armand was acutely aware of Voss's formidable reputation—a man known not only for his philanthropy but also for his relentless pursuit of rare collectibles, often weaving his way through the complexities of various industries to satiate his desires. Armand's instincts cautioned him of the potential complexities in intertwining his professional relationships with Voss's ambitious projects. He studied Voss, taking in the earnest look on his face, trying to discern the layers beneath this generous offer.

"Elliot," Armand replied guardedly, his voice measured, "your offer is most generous, and your commitment to historical preservation is indeed commendable. However, such collaborations are delicate matters, particularly involving institutions as venerable as the Vatican. I must consider this carefully, ensuring that any involvement would be in the best interest of all parties, without compromising the sanctity or the confidentiality of the archives."

Voss nodded, seemingly understanding the delicacy of the situation, but his eyes still held a spark of undeterred resolve. Armand sipped his coffee, the warmth of the drink doing little to ease the chill of apprehension that had settled over him.

Voss, sensing the hesitancy in Armand's tone, leaned in slightly, his expression earnest yet underscored by a steely determination that hinted at his unwillingness to easily relinquish his objectives. He clasped his hands together, resting them on the mahogany desk that gleamed under the soft light of the study's antique lamps.

"Armand, I understand your concerns, truly," Voss continued, his voice smooth and persuasive. "And I respect the delicate nature of any engagement with the Vatican and its archives. However, I'm proposing a substantial donation—tens of millions of dollars toward the expansion and technological enhancement of the Secret Archives." He smiled slightly as he hit on the very concept he knew worried the Baron. "This isn't about adding to my collection; it's about preserving our global heritage with the most advanced resources available."

He paused, allowing his proposal to resonate in the

opulent space between them. "Imagine the new research opportunities and the enhanced preservation techniques that such funding could support. All I ask is for an introduction to Father Dominic. I'm certain he and I share the same vision of safeguarding these treasures for the future."

Armand took another slow sip of his coffee, buying time as he mulled over Voss's words. The proposal was indeed generous and could significantly benefit Michael and his archives. Yet the baron's intuition nagged at him —Voss was a man of immense capabilities and influence, and his interests were rarely purely altruistic.

"Elliot…" Armand finally spoke, his voice carrying a diplomatic tone tinged with caution. "Your vision is commendable, and your donation's potential benefits could indeed be transformative for the Vatican and its archives."

The baron put his cup down and folded his hands on the desk, mirroring Voss's posture of negotiation. "I will propose a meeting with Father Dominic, but it should be understood this remains an initial discussion only. I am sure you recognize that thorough vetting of your proposal by the appropriate channels within the Vatican would be necessary beyond any preliminary discussions."

Voss's eyes lit up with a mixture of appreciation and calculation. "Of course, Armand. A preliminary meeting is all I ask. I'm confident that once Father Dominic understands the scope and sincerity of my proposal, he will see the potential benefits for what they are."

Armand nodded, albeit with an internal reservation

that remained unvoiced. "Very well, Elliot. I will reach out to Michael and arrange for you both to meet."

As Frederic silently collected the coffee cups, a subtle but victorious grin played across Voss's lips. Beside him, Armand bore a contemplative expression, acutely aware of the gravity and historical implications of the conversation that had just unfolded. The atmosphere was charged with a strategic tension that was both invigorating and daunting.

The gentle click of the suite's main entrance door echoed through the room, drawing Frederic's attention as he was about to pass through the foyer. Turning toward the sound, he was greeted by the sight of Hana Sinclair, whose entrance was marked by her radiant smile and confident stride.

"*Buongiorno*, Frederic," she greeted with her usual charm, her voice brightening the room. "Is Grand-père available?"

Frederic returned her smile, always uplifted by Hana's presence. "Good day, Ms. Hana," he replied warmly. "He's in the study, just wrapping up a meeting. Would you like me to announce your arrival?"

"No need, Frederic. I'll wait for the right moment to join him," she said, her voice carrying a mix of respect and familial affection.

The gleaming mahogany doors of the study swung open, revealing Armand and his distinguished guest, apparently wrapping up a deep conversation. Upon seeing Hana, Armand's expression immediately brightened with surprise and joy. He waved her over with an enthusiastic gesture.

"Ah, *ma petite* Hana!" Armand exclaimed with warm affection. "I don't believe you've had the pleasure of meeting one of our esteemed board members. Elliot Voss, this is my granddaughter, Hana Sinclair."

Hana stepped forward, extending her hand with poised confidence. "Mr. Voss, I've heard quite a bit about you through the media. It's truly a pleasure to finally meet you. I hope I'm not interrupting anything important?"

Voss, momentarily taken aback by her forthright approach yet clearly impressed, grasped her hand with a firm, respectful handshake. "Not at all, Ms. Sinclair," he replied, his eyes reflecting a spark of interest. "In fact, your grandfather and I were just discussing some fascinating aspects of the bank's historical investments."

Hana's eyes lit up, her intellectual curiosity piqued. "Oh, history is a passion of mine as well, especially when intertwined with the nuances of finance and art. Do you find that historical understanding aids in your decision-making processes for the bank?"

"You could say that," Voss answered, his voice carrying a hint of admiration for her query. "History isn't just about learning from the past, but about understanding the patterns that shape our future decisions. For instance, your grandfather mentioned earlier that you recently visited the Louvre. Did anything in particular catch your eye?"

"Yes, actually: the Near Eastern Antiquities exhibit," Hana replied, her tone animated. "It's fascinating how those ancient economies influenced today's financial systems."

Voss nodded thoughtfully. "Absolutely, the lineage of economic systems is profoundly shaped by those ancient trades and treaties. It's interesting you note that —it's rare to meet someone who connects those dots as clearly."

Hana smiled, appreciative of the depth of the conversation. "It seems we have a shared interest in looking beyond the surface, Mr. Voss."

"Indeed, Ms. Sinclair," Voss acknowledged with a slight tilt of his head. "Understanding the layers beneath the surface always reveals more than the initial glance might suggest. And please, call me Elliot."

"In that case, it's Hana," she said, shaking his hand again as she smiled. "Perhaps we'll meet again soon?"

"Yes, I'd like that very much," he replied, holding her gaze just a bit longer.

As Voss excused himself to depart, Hana felt a ripple of intrigue and a sense that their intellectual exchange had merely scratched the surface.

Her grandfather watched, a knowing smile playing on his lips as the seeds of a compelling dialogue had been sown between two keen minds. However, he recognized, too, a potential spark beyond the intellect between these two young people, both important in his life: Hana, his beloved granddaughter, and Voss, a formidable man who had just set the stage for complicating the already complex world of antiquities and finance.

CHAPTER

FOUR

The sun was just beginning to cast a warm glow over Rome, ushering in a fresh spring morning as Michael Dominic, still invigorated from his early run, joined Hana at their favorite spot, Caffè Pergamino, as previously arranged. The quaint spot, nestled on a bustling Roman street a couple of blocks from the Vatican, was alive with the murmurs of locals and the clinking of coffee cups. They found a quiet table outside, shaded by an ancient elm tree, and settled in with their coffee.

Hana was animated, her eyes sparkling with the recount of last night's encounter. "So there I was at Grand-père's, and out walks this remarkably charismatic man—Elliot Voss. Oh, Michael, he's not just accomplished but also quite charming and, dare I say, rather good-looking."

Michael, who was sipping his espresso, nearly choked on it as realization dawned on him. "Elliot Voss!

That's where I know him from! Of course, one of the richest men in the world," he exclaimed, setting his cup down with a clatter. "He was the one who stood up during that presentation I gave last week, asking about St. Peter's bones. I knew he looked familiar."

"Oh, you've met him then!" Hana said, her interest piqued as she leaned in closer. "He didn't mention it. But then, it was only a brief meeting. He was leaving just as I entered."

Michael's brow furrowed slightly, a twinge of jealousy creeping into his tone. "Well, we didn't exactly meet, but he does seem to have a knack for making a memorable impression," he said dryly. "But there's something about his question that day… it was too pointed, almost probing. It makes you wonder what his real interests are."

Hana laughed softly, brushing off his concerns. "Oh, Michael, you always are suspicious. Maybe he's just a history buff, you know? And besides, his attention to detail is quite… flattering."

"Flattering, huh?" Michael replied, the word tasting a bit sour as he tried to mask his unease with a forced smile. "Just be careful, Hana. People with massive resources like Voss often have agendas that aren't so charming up close."

Hana reached across the table, giving his hand a reassuring squeeze. "I will. But for now, let's just enjoy this beautiful day in the world's most amazing city." Her laughter echoed slightly, blending with the sounds of the waking city, as Michael managed a genuine smile, his worries momentarily eased by her lightheartedness.

IN THE HEART of Vatican City, the Fabbrica di San Pietro —the office tasked with the upkeep, maintenance, and administration of St. Peter's Basilica—buzzed with a sense of historic anticipation. This year marked the 1100th anniversary of the discovery and resanctification of St. Peter's bones, an event of profound significance to the Catholic world. Monsignor Matteo Ferrante, a man known for his deep reverence for Church history and meticulous attention to detail, had been planning the celebration for months. Appointed by the pope to lead this momentous celebration, he had been coordinating closely with Father Dominic's office in the Secret Archives to ensure the event honored the sacredness and the historical importance of the relics.

Monsignor Ferrante scrutinized the sprawling blueprint of St. Peter's Basilica spread across his desk, including the Vatican Grottoes with their subterranean papal crypts and the entire basilica complex. Ferrante's office was cluttered with documents: liturgical texts, guest lists, and ceremonial outlines. As he answered a call, the walls echoed slightly with the sounds of early preparations outside where a special chapel was being constructed.

"Good morning, Monsignor. Michael Dominic here," came the voice from the other end once he picked up. "How are things going?"

"Father Dominic, I'm so glad you called. I'm looking at the procession route now. The celebration is to commence with a grand cortège through the Vatican, starting from the Apostolic Palace and winding its way to the basilica. The relics of St. Peter will be carried in a magnificently adorned reliquary, flanked by the Swiss Guards in their striking uniforms and a procession of clergy in vibrant vestments. And the air will be filled with the solemn melodies of the Sistine Chapel Choir, enhancing the spiritual ambience.

"We're coordinating with the Swiss Guards on security arrangements. They're training this week," Ferrante explained further, his voice rich with a mix of duty and anticipation.

"That's excellent news," Father Dominic replied. "And the choir? Are the new hymns coming along for the procession?"

"Yes, they've started rehearsals. It promises to be spiritually enriching," Ferrante affirmed, his eyes wandering to the window where the sounds of the choir filtered in, their melodies floating above the disciplined march of the Swiss Guards in the courtyard below.

FERRANTE LATER MET with Pope Clement in a quiet, sunlit corner of the Vatican Gardens. They discussed the intricacies of the celebration over a small, ancient wooden table.

"Upon reaching the basilica, Holy Father, you would preside over a special Mass, attended by tens of thousands of pilgrims from around the world, as well as numerous cardinals and bishops. As I understand it, your homily will reflect on the enduring legacy of St. Peter as the first pope and the cornerstone of the

Church, highlighting the themes of continuity, faith, and divine guidance.

"Then, following the Mass, Your Holiness will bless the relics before they're placed on public display in a specially constructed, climate-controlled chapel tent on the steps of the basilica. This chapel, designed under my guidance, will feature intricate mosaics depicting scenes from St. Peter's life, crafted by some of Italy's finest artists."

Ferrante went on to describe that throughout the day there would be scholarly presentations and discussions in the adjacent halls, featuring prominent theologians and historians speaking on the significance of St. Peter's legacy. These sessions would be open to the public, providing a deeper understanding of the historical and spiritual importance of the relics.

The event was designed to resonate far beyond the walls of the Vatican, its majesty and solemnity broadcast live to millions around the globe. Cutting-edge video and audio technology had been meticulously installed to capture every sacred moment, ensuring the celebration's profound significance would touch hearts in every corner of the world.

The pope sat in quiet reflection, his fingers brushing the worn edges of his homily notes. "This is more than a commemoration of St. Peter," he said, his voice firm yet imbued with hope. "At a time when the world is fractured by division and doubt, we must offer a beacon of faith and unity. Let this moment rekindle devotion in the hearts of the faithful and remind the world of the Church's enduring mission. If we succeed, this can be a renewal not only of spirit but also of commitment—strengthening our community and the Church's ability to serve." He paused, gazing at Ferrante intently. "Let us make this a turning point, one that draws the faithful closer and inspires those seeking answers to find them in Christ and His Church."

As FERRANTE RETURNED to his office, he paused to observe the preparations outside once more. The Swiss Guards perfected their formations, and the choir's voices soared. In these moments, the weight of the upcoming celebration seemed both monumental and profoundly inspiring.

Sharing a brief update with Father Dominic on another call, Ferrante's voice carried a quiet confidence. "Father, we're shaping an event that I believe will resonate deeply within the hearts of all who attend."

Michael's response was warm and supportive. "Matteo, it sounds like we are indeed ready to offer a tapestry of faith and history. Let's keep this momentum going. We're not just planning an event; we're preparing a milestone."

Ferrante ended the call, a sense of responsibility and anticipation settling over him as he looked again at the basilica's outlines. Each line on the plans was more than just a guide for the celebration—it was a blueprint for a moment in history, soon to be woven into the fabric of the Church's legacy.

CHAPTER

FIVE

I n the elegantly appointed living room of Armand de Saint-Clair's apartment atop the Rome Cavalieri, Michael Dominic stood by the expansive window. His gaze lingered on the city skyline, where the dome of St. Peter's Basilica etched a solemn silhouette against the fading evening light. The room, lit by a delicate crystal chandelier, exuded a sense of quiet luxury, with its plush furnishings and refined decor bridging Old World charm and contemporary opulence.

Armand approached Michael with two glasses of red wine in hand, the light reflecting softly off the polished crystal. "I appreciate you coming on such short notice, Michael," he said, offering one of the glasses to his guest.

"Thank you, Baron. Your hospitality is always so generous," the priest replied with a slight smile, accepting the glass.

As the sound of the doorbell echoed through the apartment, Armand excused himself with a courteous nod and strode toward the entrance. Opening the door, he welcomed Elliot Voss—a figure of unmistakable charisma and ambition. Voss's presence filled the room as he stepped inside, his tailored suit a testament to his affluence and meticulous attention to detail.

"Elliot, welcome. Please, do come in," Armand said, extending his hand.

Voss stepped inside, his eyes quickly settling on Michael. "Elliot, allow me to introduce you to Father Michael Dominic, Prefect of the Vatican Apostolic Archives," Armand continued, indicating Michael, who had turned from the window to meet their guest.

Voss smiled warmly, extending his hand to the priest. "Father Dominic, it's a pleasure to finally meet you."

Michael shook Voss's hand. "Mr. Voss, the pleasure is mine."

They moved to the seating area, and Armand offered Voss a drink, which he declined with a polite wave.

"Father Dominic," Voss began, leaning slightly forward, "I've heard remarkable things about your work with the archives. It's truly inspiring. And please, it's Elliot."

"Thank you, Elliot. We strive to preserve and protect the history entrusted to us," Michael replied modestly.

"That's precisely why I'm here," Voss said, clearly enthusiastic. "As an armchair historian myself, I believe in the importance of your mission and would like to support it."

Armand took a seat beside Michael, listening intently.

"Coming straight to the point, I've arranged for a grant of fifty million dollars to help expand and upgrade your archives," Voss continued. "Think of the possibilities, Father—enhanced preservation methods, digitalization of ancient texts, even new facilities and expanded staff."

Michael's eyes widened slightly in surprise. He took a moment to compose his thoughts, with a glance at Armand. When the baron had suggested to Michael that he meet with Voss, he hadn't hinted at the reason behind the introduction. Michael noted the baron's guarded expression, then turned back to the would-be benefactor. "That's an incredibly generous offer, Elliot. The archives would benefit greatly from such support."

"In fact, I have given this much thought and have an additional benefit to attach to my offer," Voss added, his tone shifting slightly.

Michael's gaze sharpened. "And what benefit might that be?"

"I wish to assist in the forthcoming celebration of St. Peter's bones. My team and I have some ideas that could make the event truly spectacular, drawing global attention to the Vatican," Voss explained.

Michael exchanged a quick glance with Armand, who looked equally intrigued and cautious. "The celebration of St. Peter's bones is a deeply significant event for the Church. Any involvement would need to be carefully considered," Michael said thoughtfully.

Voss leaned back, exuding confidence. "Of course.

I'm not looking to overstep any boundaries. I simply want to contribute in a meaningful way. With our combined efforts, we can make this an unforgettable occasion."

Michael took a deep breath, the weight of the decision evident in his expression. "What are your thoughts on this, Baron?" he asked, turning to Armand.

"To my knowledge, Elliot's offer is unprecedented," Armand replied calmly. "However, we must ensure that any collaboration aligns with the Church's values and traditions."

"I assure you, my intentions are to enhance and support, not to disrupt. Together, I believe we can achieve something truly remarkable," Voss said sincerely.

Michael sat back, weighing the offer and the potential implications. Thinking back to his recent presentation and Voss's curious interest in the bones then wasn't lost on him. "I'll need some time to discuss this with my superiors and consider all aspects. But I appreciate your offer, Elliot, and your interest in our work."

Voss nodded. "Take whatever time you need, Father Dominic. I look forward to the possibility of our working together. Starting with the current preparations for St. Peter's celebration, of course."

With that, Voss rose from his seat, his eyes meeting Michael's. He extended his hand once more to the priest. "Thank you for your time and consideration, Father. I know you will make the right decision for the Church."

Michael shook Voss's hand firmly, "Indeed, Elliot. And, either way, thank you again for your generous offer."

Armand, too, had risen to his feet. "Elliot, let me show you out," he offered. They disappeared into the labyrinthine apartment, leaving Michael alone in the luxurious sitting room filled with antique furniture and masterpieces of Renaissance art.

Alone with his thoughts, Michael held onto the crystal glass half-filled with wine. He was intrigued by Voss's proposition but also wary. Voss was known for his charm and efficiency but whispers about his ruthless ambition were just as prevalent in elite circles.

Yet... fifty million dollars? Michael knew such resources would revolutionize their operations at the Vatican Archives. The possibilities were indeed exciting. However, bringing in such a powerful figure could also disrupt the careful balance within the Church's event staffing hierarchy.

A few minutes later Armand returned, closing the heavy door behind him. His usually calm face seemed slightly tensed now. "Michael," he began cautiously, "I think we need to tread carefully here."

Michael nodded in agreement, his brow furrowed as he continued to contemplate their situation. "Yes... and it worries me how much interest he has shown in St. Peter's bones... one of our most valued relics. This is the second time he's brought them up to me." He explained Voss's appearance at his recent presentation.

"Now that's interesting," Armand noted.

They fell into silence, each lost in their own

thoughts. The room was shrouded in darkness now; only the faint glow from a single lamp illuminated their faces.

"Yes, I agree," the priest reaffirmed, swirling the wine in his glass thoughtfully. "Though it could potentially bring many positive changes, his offer is as sudden as it is generous. Still, we shouldn't rush into anything without thorough deliberation." Michael knew firsthand the lengthy delays that ensued any time a decision was required of the Church hierarchy. Yet Voss had made clear his offer was coupled with the upcoming event to be held soon. To say this would require a fast-track decision of the Church was an understatement in itself.

"I concur," Armand said, pouring himself another glass of wine. "Elliot's reputation precedes him as well. We need to consider all aspects before allowing him a stake in our sacred traditions."

"Absolutely," Michael mused aloud. "The preservation of our history cannot be compromised by any secular pursuits."

The two men nodded at each other in agreement, their thoughts revolving around the magnitude of the decision that lay ahead. It was now up to Michael to navigate these choppy waters without rocking the vessel that had safeguarded the Church's history for centuries.

CHAPTER

SIX

Elliot Voss sat alone in the study of his sprawling rented villa on the outskirts of Rome, the walls lined with shelves of antique books and artifacts that spoke of his obsession with history and its treasures. The glow of his laptop computer illuminated his face as he scrutinized a collection of photographs sprawled across the mahogany desk. These were no ordinary images; they were high-resolution photographs of St. Peter's bones, taken from various angles and with exceptional detail, released by the Vatican over the years for scholarly review. There weren't many bones in the official display case—a jeweled box inside an ornately fashioned bronze reliquary—but what remained—nine small bone fragments befitting an old man in his sixties—were venerated nonetheless.

Voss's eyes, sharp and calculating, moved meticulously from one image to another, his mind weaving through the nuances of each bone's contour and texture. The room was silent, save for the occasional sip he took from a glass of aged whiskey, the ice clinking softly against the glass.

He leaned back in his chair, thoughtfully tapping a silver pen against his lips. "To replicate such sacred relics... precision would be key," he murmured to himself. His plan was audacious, bordering on sacrilegious, but his determination was fueled by more than mere curiosity; it was driven by a need to hold power over something as untouchable as the Vatican's secrets. And to acquire the key to the greatest of humanity's secrets: immortality.

THE NEXT MORNING, Voss met with a Canadian expat working in Rome: Dr. Helena Barrett, a renowned authority in ancient relics who possessed an uncanny ability to restore or recreate historical artifacts with astonishing accuracy. They convened in a private room of a discreet café in Trastevere, a place chosen for its anonymity.

Barrett, a woman in her early fifties, carried herself with an air of quiet authority that seemed to fill every room she entered. Her keen, steel-gray eyes were sharp and discerning, always seeming to assess and categorize everything—and everyone—with a precision honed by years of meticulous academic research. Framed by a cascade of dark brown hair streaked tastefully with silver, her features were strikingly symmetrical, the kind that conveyed both intellect and elegance. High cheekbones and a faintly pointed chin lent her an aristocratic profile, while her poised demeanor suggested a woman accustomed to being listened to, even in rooms dominated by powerful men.

Dr. Barrett listened intently as Voss laid out his plan. Her expression was unreadable, one finger idly tapping a cup of black coffee nestled between her hands.

"You understand the complexity and the delicacy of what I'm asking?" Voss inquired, his tone serious, measuring the weight of his request.

Barrett nodded, her mind already turning over the ethical implications and technical challenges. "Creating a precise replica of ancient bones is not only about getting the shape and size right," she said carefully. "It's about aging, patina, microscopic details that suggest many centuries of existence. It's about creating a forgery that could fool even the most seasoned archaeologists." The challenge intrigued her but the ramifications made her hesitate.

Voss slid a folder across the table toward her. Inside were the photographs, along with a generous upfront payment and an offer of resources that few in her field could ever hope to access.

"This isn't just a job, Dr. Barrett. It's the project of a lifetime," Voss urged, watching her closely.

Barrett paused, the moral crossroads clear in her mind, yet the challenge was irresistibly compelling. And the fee outstanding. Finally, she closed the folder, her decision made. "I'll need complete autonomy and discretion. And understand this, Mr. Voss: we are not just replicating a set of bones. We are venturing into a realm where science and sacrilege tread a fine line."

Voss's smile was thin and satisfied. "That's exactly why I came to you, Helena."

HELENA BARRETT'S lab processes employed a combination of 3D imaging and traditional sculpting techniques, consulting with forensic anthropologists and bioarchaeologists to ensure every microscopic detail was replicated—right down to the most minute textural nuances that hinted at the bones' age-old origins.

Each step was a labor of patience and precision, with Barrett often working late into the night, her workshop lit by the focused beam of task lights, casting long shadows on the walls lined with her tools and materials. The bones slowly took shape, emerging from blocks of specially formulated materials that mimicked the density and fragility of human bone.

As she held up a nearly finished thoracic vertebra against the light, examining it through a magnifying loupe, she couldn't help but feel a twinge of unease at the paradox of her task—creating a false relic destined to challenge truths held sacred for millennia. Yet in the silent communion with her craft, she found a strange reverence, not for the deceit it represented, but for the artistry it demanded.

Back in his study, Voss waited impatiently for the completion of the project, the pieces of his greater scheme slowly falling into place, each step forward tightening his grip on the power he sought so relentlessly.

In the quiet sanctum of his office, with the muffled whispers of history rustling through shelves lined with leather-bound volumes, Michael Dominic sat across from Hana Sinclair. The afternoon sun filtered through stained glass, casting colorful patterns across the ornate carpet. She had come at his request, a need for a trusted ear for the quandary he faced.

Michael's hands were clasped on the mahogany desk as he regarded Hana with a look of concern. "Voss's offer is generous, without doubt; fifty million dollars could do much for the archives. But his conditions…" His voice trailed off, his brow furrowed in contemplation.

Hana leaned forward, her eyes bright with a mix of determination and persuasion. "Michael, think about what this means beyond the money. Elliot Voss isn't just a businessman; he's a visionary. His involvement could bring a level of public attention and acclaim to the Vatican's efforts that we've never seen before."

Michael sighed, the weight of his role as the Prefect of the Vatican Archives heavy upon his shoulders. "It's precisely that kind of attention that worries me. The celebration of St. Peter's bones is a sacred event. Having someone like Voss, who views this through the lens of spectacle rather than sanctity..."

"But isn't your goal to share the Church's treasures with the world?" Hana interjected, her tone gentle yet firm. "To educate and inspire faith? Elliot can help you reach corners of the globe you can't on your own. His network, his resources—imagine the possibilities, Michael."

The priest leaned back in his chair, the leather creaking softly. He looked out the window at the Vatican Gardens, a serene oasis that seemed worlds away from the storm of decisions raging in his mind. "And what of our independence? Our tradition?" he asked, turning back to look at her. "We've always safeguarded our heritage from secular influences. Isn't there a risk that we might dilute our very essence for broader appeal?"

Hana nodded, acknowledging his concerns with a respectful tilt of her head. "There is always a risk, I suppose. But consider this—Voss is offering a bridge, not a takeover. You lead the project; you set the boundaries. You keep the sanctity intact while embracing a chance to illuminate the Church's history in ways you've never tried before."

Michael's gaze drifted to a small crucifix on his desk,

the symbol of steadfast faith and sacrifice. After a moment of silent reflection, he met Hana's gaze again. "I want to believe that we can do this without compromising what we stand for. Maybe…" His voice softened. "Maybe it's time we open the doors just a bit wider, with the right safeguards in place, of course."

Hana's expression brightened, a spark of relief mingling with excitement. "I truly believe this is a step forward, Michael. Let's navigate this together. We'll ensure the archives and its legacies are honored—not just displayed."

As the light in the room grew golden with the late afternoon sun, Michael offered a tentative smile, the decision made, yet the journey ahead uncertain. "All right. Let's draft a proposal for Mr. Voss, one that respects our values and embraces potential. We'll tread this new path with caution, guided by faith."

Hana's face relaxed into a warm smile. "Wise consideration, Michael. I'm sure you won't regret it." She rose from her seat, extending a hand across the desk.

Michael accepted it, his warm grip firm and steady. "Well, I trust your instincts, but let's just ensure our faith isn't misplaced."

Hana suggested, "You can use the Vatican legal counsel to ensure all the 'i's are dotted on the proposal for an extra measure of comfort."

Michael nodded. As Hana left the office, Michael remained seated, his gaze once again captured by the small crucifix on his desk. He reached out, his fingers brushing against the cold metal symbol of suffering. A heavy sigh escaped his lips—a sigh of relief, with some fear and anticipation for what was to come.

In the ensuing days, Michael carefully drafted a proposal, aided by the Vatican's legal department, that delicately balanced tradition with innovation. Voss's involvement would be strictly controlled under the Vatican's terms; any transgression would lead to an immediate severance of ties, while retaining the millions in grant money.

THE AFTERNOON LIGHT streamed through the high windows of Monsignor Matteo Ferrante's office, illuminating the intricate details of the ancient frescoes that adorned the walls. Michael Dominic stepped inside, the air heavy with the scent of aged paper and incense. Ferrante stood behind his desk, his expression a mix of welcome and worry as he looked down at Voss's proposal.

"Good morning, Michael," Ferrante greeted, extending his hand across the cluttered expanse of his desk. "I trust you've considered the ramifications of this proposal?"

Michael nodded, taking the offered seat. "I have, Matteo. I know it's unorthodox, but Elliot Voss's offer could significantly benefit the archives and our mission."

Ferrante sighed, leaning back in his chair, his fingers steepled. "Michael, my concern isn't about the monetary gain. It's the precedent it sets. Voss is a secular figure, a businessman. His involvement could be seen as a commercialization of our sacred traditions."

Michael listened intently, recognizing the gravity of Ferrante's concerns. "I understand your worries, I do. But consider the state of our archives. This funding could preserve and digitize countless documents, making our history more accessible to the faithful around the world. Isn't our mission to share our heritage?"

Ferrante's gaze shifted toward a crucifix hanging on the wall, his brow furrowed. "And what of our autonomy? Are we to dance to the tune of every donor with deep pockets?"

"Elliot Voss won't be pulling any strings," Michael assured him, his voice firm. "We've drafted a restrictive contract here, Matteo. He must agree to our terms, our supervision. He doesn't shape the event; he merely helps facilitate it."

"And you believe he will agree to this?" Ferrante questioned, skepticism lining his tone.

"I do. He seems passionate about making a positive impact. And we make it clear—any deviation from our agreed terms, and the deal is off—while we retain the entire grant funding. Our legal counsel has helped me draft the contract with the strictest of terms." Michael's resolve was palpable. "It's a controlled opening, one that allows us to maintain our sacredness while still embracing a chance to expand our reach."

Ferrante considered this, his eyes drifting to the window where the city of Rome lay beyond, a testament to centuries of faith and tradition. After a long moment, he turned back to Michael, his decision clear. "I will trust your judgment on this, Father. I want every contingency accounted for."

Michael's expression softened, relieved by Ferrante's conditional support. "It has been. Thank you, Matteo. I promise we'll move forward with the utmost caution. This could be a new chapter for us, one that honors our past while securing our future."

As Michael left Ferrante's office, the weight of their conversation lingered for the priest. The potential for great good was there, but so too was the risk. Now, more than ever, Michael felt the burden of his responsibilities, poised at the crossroads of tradition and progress.

VOSS'S RESPONSE arrived after several anxious days of waiting in the form of a crisp white envelope bearing his personal seal—his full acceptance of their conditions handwritten on a single sheet of paper.

A sense of both triumph and concern filled Michael as he read Voss's agreement. Triumph because they had successfully negotiated terms that safeguarded the Church's traditions while opening up new possibilities; concern because it marked the beginning of an unfamiliar path strewn with unknown challenges.

The sun began to set over St. Peter's Square, the silhouette of the basilica standing tall against the vibrant hues of dusk. As Michael looked out from his office window, he was filled with renewed determination to lead his team, face any storm, and uphold the sanctity of the Church's heritage. They were embarking on an uncertain journey, but they would tread cautiously, guided by unwavering faith.

EIGHT

The Cortile d'Onore, or Courtyard of Honor nestled within the Vatican's fortified walls, was alive with the precise and regimented movements of the Swiss Guards. Karl Dengler, a seasoned officer with a sharp eye for detail, stood at the edge of the courtyard, his stern gaze sweeping over the assembled guards. Beside him, Lukas Bischoff, younger but no less dedicated, mirrored his superior's intensity, both men embodying the discipline and tradition of their elite corps.

Today's practice was no ordinary drill. The upcoming ceremony to honor St. Peter's bones was a significant event, not just for the Vatican but for the entire Catholic world. The stakes were high and, as always for such major occasions, the possibility of threats—ranging from coordinated terrorist attacks to lone gunmen—required meticulous preparation.

"Formation A!" Karl barked, his voice echoing off

the ancient walls. The guards snapped into a defensive perimeter, their halberds gleaming under the bright Roman sun. Each movement was synchronized, a testament to their rigorous training and unyielding discipline.

Lukas nodded approvingly, his hands clasped behind his back. "Good. But remember, the real threat won't give us time to think. We need to react instinctively. Again, but faster this time."

The guards reset, their faces masks of concentration. They moved through the drill again, quicker this time, their actions a blur of coordinated efficiency.

"Now, let's simulate a lone gunman," Karl instructed, his tone grave. "This time, he emerges from the crowd in St. Peter's Square."

A guard stepped forward, playing the role of the attacker. He mimicked drawing a weapon, and in an instant, the Swiss Guards sprang into action. Shields were raised, halberds pointed, and a protective barrier was formed around the imagined VIP.

"Hold!" Lukas shouted, his eyes keenly observing every movement. "Karl, did you see the gap on the left flank?"

Karl nodded, a rare frown creasing his forehead. "I did. We can't afford any mistakes."

"Again, and this time, close that gap," Lukas called out, pointing to the left.

The guards repeated the drill, their movements even more precise, the gap in the formation now seamlessly closed.

"Better," Karl acknowledged, "but we need to be perfect. Let's move on to the terrorist scenario."

This drill was more complex. It involved multiple attackers and required the guards to shift from defensive to offensive maneuvers seamlessly. The guards formed a tight phalanx, then split into smaller units to neutralize the threats.

"Keep your eyes on the crowd," Lukas reminded them. "Assume everyone is a potential threat. No hesitation."

The guards moved with lethal efficiency, their actions a choreographed dance of protection and precision. Each scenario was played out to its fullest, every detail scrutinized and perfected.

As the sun began to dip, throwing long shadows across the courtyard, Karl and Lukas called the guards to attention. "Good work today," Karl said, his tone softer but still authoritative. "But remember, our duty is not just to protect the pope and the Vatican. We are the last line of defense for something much larger. St. Peter's bones represent the very foundation of our faith. We cannot fail."

Lukas nodded, stepping forward. "Tomorrow, we drill again. And the day after. Until we're not just ready, but beyond ready. Dismissed."

The guards saluted, their faces showing a mix of exhaustion and determination. As they dispersed, Karl and Lukas exchanged a glance, a silent agreement passing between them. They knew the importance of their task and the weight of responsibility that rested on their shoulders. The ceremony honoring St. Peter's remains would proceed with the full might and vigilance of the Swiss Guards ensuring its sanctity and safety.

THE LATE AFTERNOON sun filtered through the arched windows of Helena Barrett's home laboratory, casting long, golden rays over the gleaming countertops and cluttered workspace. The room was an eclectic blend of precision and chaos: calibrated microscopes and spectrometers stood side by side with stacks of aged manuscripts and jars of curious chemicals. In the center of it all was Helena, meticulously bent over a bone fragment held delicately in gloved hands. A soft hum of classical music played in the background, though she barely noticed it, her mind consumed by calculations and doubt.

Nearby, a folder filled with notes and sketches lay open, the pages scattered with intricate diagrams and detailed observations about bone structures and aging techniques. Helena glanced at the paperwork with a flicker of hesitation. She had brought it here to weigh her options—whether to move forward with the next step of this fraught commission or find a way to extricate herself entirely.

Her deliberation was interrupted by a sharp knock at the heavy oak door. Startled, Helena carefully set the fragment down on a padded tray and stripped off her gloves. When she opened the door, Dr. Emilio Rossi stood there, a tall man with a weathered face and sharp eyes that always seemed to miss nothing.

"Dr. Barrett," he greeted warmly, extending his hand. "I hope I'm not intruding, but I had a proposition I thought might intrigue you."

Helena hesitated for a moment before ushering him inside. "Of course, Emilio. Please, come in."

As they entered the lab, Emilio's gaze swept across the room, drawn to the assortment of tools and notes scattered across the workstation. Helena quickly moved to close the folder, but not before Emilio caught sight of a detailed sketch of a bone fragment, annotated with dates and aging data and the words "St. Peter."

He raised an eyebrow. "Working on something special, are we?" he asked, his tone light but curious. "Looks like bones. Vatican commission, perhaps? A replica for one of their exhibitions?"

Helena stiffened, her hands resting protectively on the folder. "Just a private commission," she said curtly, avoiding his eyes.

Emilio's curiosity turned into excitement. "Helena, if the Vatican has you working on something like this, it could be monumental! You must tell me more."

"It's not what you think," she replied quickly, her voice a little too sharp. "It's nothing to do with the Vatican. Just an ordinary project for a private collector."

His excitement gave way to suspicion, and his eyes narrowed as he studied her. "Ordinary? A woman like you doesn't take on 'ordinary' projects. And you're nervous—unusual for someone as collected as you. What's going on?"

Helena's lips pressed into a thin line. "I don't owe you an explanation, Emilio. You know how these private commissions work—confidentiality is part of the deal."

He leaned closer, lowering his voice. "Helena, I've worked with the Church long enough to know that meddling with relics—even reproductions—is dangerous territory. If this isn't sanctioned by the Vatican, you could be stepping into something far more serious than you realize."

"I'm not 'meddling' with anything," she shot back, but her voice wavered.

He folded his arms, unconvinced. "Even if it's not the Church, handling artifacts like this without full transparency can ruin careers—yours and whoever hired you. And if it is Vatican property you're working on, unauthorized, the consequences could be… severe." He softened slightly. "You're brilliant, Helena, but brilliance won't protect you from the fallout if you're not careful."

Her face paled slightly, but she forced a small, brittle smile. "Thank you for your concern, Emilio. I assure you, I know what I'm doing."

Emilio didn't look convinced, but he nodded slowly. "I hope so. You've always been one of the best in the field, Helena. I'd hate to see that brilliance overshadowed by a… mistake."

"You mentioned something about a proposition, Emilio? To be honest, I cannot entertain anything else at the moment," Helena said sharply. "Might we discuss this at some other time? I've got a pressing time commitment here…"

Emilio paused. "Of course, Helena, it can wait." He glanced once more at the folder before stepping toward the door. "In the meantime, be careful. For your sake."

As the door closed behind him, Helena let out a shaky breath, her composure momentarily cracking. Her eyes drifted back to the bone fragment on the tray, its surface gleaming under the lamplight. With trembling hands, she picked it up again, but her mind was racing. Emilio had seen too much, and now she wasn't sure how much longer she could keep this quiet.

NINE

The air was cool and slightly musty, carrying the scent of ancient stone and earth. Dim lights cast shadows across the narrow passageways, illuminating the path with a soft, golden hue. Marcus Russo, the Vatican's chief archaeologist, knelt carefully beside a partially uncovered sarcophagus, his gloved hands meticulously brushing away centuries of accumulated dust. The mausoleums beneath St. Peter's Basilica, a labyrinthine network of burial chambers and sacred spaces, had been his second home for years. He and his staff had just begun their meticulous efforts on a yet uncatalogued area under the basilica.

A scholarly man just north of fifty years old, Marcus possessed an air of quiet intensity. His close-cropped dark hair, now flecked with silver, framed a face that bore the signs of a life spent in study and discovery. His hazel eyes, sharp and focused, reflected the glint of his lamp as he examined the carvings on the stone before him. Each line and curve held meaning, each symbol a piece of a much larger puzzle that he had devoted his life to solving.

Marcus had been recruited by the Vatican straight out of the University of Rome, where he had completed his doctorate in archaeology with a focus on Early Christian relics. His thesis on the early martyrdoms in Rome had caught the attention of the Church's higher echelons, and he had quickly become one of the Vatican's most trusted experts. Over the years, he had led numerous excavations and had been instrumental in uncovering and preserving some of the most significant Christian artifacts in history.

Today, his work was closer to home, just meters away from where the bones of St. Peter had been discovered decades earlier. The location was fraught with historical and religious significance, and Marcus felt the weight of his task with every careful scrape of his tools. He was cataloging a series of mausoleums that had been relatively untouched, possibly dating back to the second century. His team, a small but dedicated group of Vatican-appointed assistants, was working nearby, cataloging the smaller finds that dotted the same area.

"Dr. Russo," one of his assistants, a young intern named Sofia, called out, breaking the silence. She approached him cautiously, holding a small digital tablet with notes. "We've found some inscriptions on the western wall. They seem to reference early Christians, but I'm having trouble translating one of the sections. It's... most unusual."

Marcus stood, his back cracking slightly as he rose from his crouched position. He took the tablet from Sofia, his brows knitting in concentration as he reviewed the data. "Unusual how?" he asked.

"There's a phrase here that doesn't match any of the early Christian symbols we've encountered before," Sofia explained, pointing to the screen. "It almost looks like a cipher."

Marcus frowned, intrigued. His expertise was primarily in the physical excavation and preservation of artifacts, but he was no stranger to the cryptic language and codes that often accompanied such discoveries. "Let me see," he murmured, more to himself than to Sofia, as he studied the inscription closely.

The words were indeed unfamiliar, a mix of Latin and an older script that he couldn't immediately place. This was a rare find, a different script than would be expected to be here, something that could potentially reshape their understanding of the early Christian community in Rome. Could this show that other groups of people had been part of the early Church? Marcus felt a thrill of excitement stir within him—this was why he did what he did, for moments like these when history seemed to whisper directly to him.

"We'll need to get this analyzed further," he finally said, handing the tablet back to Sofia. "Contact Professor Vitale at the Pontifical Oriental Institute. She's an expert in early Christian languages. And make sure the site here is secure—whatever this is, I believe it's important."

As Sofia hurried off to follow his instructions,

Marcus turned back to the sarcophagus. He couldn't shake the feeling that this discovery was just the beginning of something much larger. What other ancient people might have worshipped here? The weight of centuries pressed in around him, but he welcomed it, feeling more alive than he had in months. This was what he lived for—the thrill of uncovering the past and the promise of what those discoveries could mean for the future.

Marcus carefully brushed more dust from the sarcophagus, revealing an intricate carving of a cross surrounded by a wreath. The style was unusual, almost Celtic in nature, unlike the starker Roman designs common in the catacombs. He leaned in, squinting in the dim light, and noted that within the wreath were etched tiny symbols, some familiar from his years of study, others strange and esoteric.

"This is no ordinary tomb," he murmured. Questions tumbled through his mind. *Who was interred here? Why were they buried so close to St. Peter's resting place? And what was the meaning behind these mysterious symbols?*

Footsteps echoed down the passageway, and Marcus turned to see Sofia returning, a troubled look on her face.

"Professor Vitale is away at a conference," Sofia reported. "Her assistant said she can't look at the inscription until next week."

Marcus nodded, frowning. Everything involving the Church, from academic calendars to discoveries under the Vatican, moved slowly compared to his desire for information.

"Very well," he said after a moment. "We'll photograph and catalog the inscription and seal this chamber so it's undisturbed until she returns. I have a feeling our friend here may be able to tell us more."

He gestured to the carved sarcophagus. Sofia looked skeptical. "How will we learn anything more without the inscription?"

Marcus gave her a cryptic smile. "By listening very closely to what the stones have to say."

Sofia looked at Marcus quizzically, unsure what he meant. As an academic, she dealt in facts and evidence, not hunches or mysticism or listening to stones.

Marcus seemed to sense her hesitation. "Come, I'll show you," he said gently, beckoning for her to join him beside the sarcophagus.

Carefully, almost reverently, he ran his hand along the carved lid, tracing the intricate Celtic designs. He closed his eyes in concentration as his fingers explored every crevice and curve. To Sofia it seemed he was reading the symbols through touch alone.

After several long moments, Marcus opened his eyes. "You see, these carvings tell a story," he explained. "This symbol here represents St. Peter. And this wreath shape is reminiscent of the crown of thorns worn by Jesus during his crucifixion."

He continued to decrypt the meanings of the symbols, piecing together an astonishing narrative of early Christian persecution and martyrdom. Sofia listened, rapt. She had always relied solely on books and scientific evidence, yet here was knowledge passed down through art, preserved in stone.

"The ancients had many ways of recording history," Marcus concluded. "If we listen closely, even the stones will speak."

Sofia felt a shiver run down her spine as she absorbed Marcus's words. The pale light of the crypt seemed to flicker, casting dancing shadows across the carved surface of the sarcophagus. She leaned in closer, her breath catching as she noticed details she had overlooked before.

"But what about this symbol here?" she asked, pointing to an intricate knot pattern near the base. "It seems different from the others."

Marcus's eyes lit up. "Ah, you have a keen eye, my dear. That particular design is indeed unique." He traced the pattern with his finger, his touch feather-light against the cool stone. "It's a variation of the Triquetra— a symbol of the Holy Trinity. But see how it's interwoven with what appears to be a key?"

Sofia nodded, her pulse quickening. "What does it mean?"

Marcus's voice dropped to a near-whisper. "I believe it represents a truth about St. Peter's role in the early Church, maybe that he is a key to the faith." For a moment he cocked his head, considering why such a symbol would be used in this way, rather than a more direct reference. "Or… to something else, but certainly significant. Maybe something that was too dangerous to record openly."

The air in the crypt seemed to grow thicker, laden with centuries of secrets. Sofia could almost feel the weight of history pressing down upon them. She glanced nervously at the shadows gathering in the corners of the room.

"Instead of waiting for Professor Vitale, do you think Father Dominic might know what the inscription means?" she asked. "I understand he's an expert in several ancient languages. We may know more if he's able to translate the inscription and confirm your theory."

Marcus nodded slowly, his eyes never leaving the sarcophagus. "Yes, good idea. We should contact him immediately then."

TEN

F ather Michael Dominic crouched low beside the ancient sarcophagus, the beam of his flashlight casting long, flickering shadows against the rough-hewn walls of the catacombs beneath St. Peter's Basilica. The air was thick, damp, and smelled of stone and dust with a centuries-old silence pressing down on him. His eyes narrowed as they followed the faint, winding script etched across the worn stone lid, its jagged lines forming unfamiliar symbols.

Next to him, Marcus and Sofia watched intently. "What do you make of it?" Marcus asked the priest, his voice hushed as if fearing to disturb the long-dead secret.

Michael's fingers traced the carved lines, the faint edges of each symbol flicking a spark of recognition in his mind. He had studied ancient languages—Celtic among them—but this was something older, a dialect that had nearly slipped through the cracks of time, forgotten by most scholars. As he worked through it, the words began to form.

"It's... Celtic, but not the standard Old Irish," Michael murmured. "This is... Brythonic, an archaic form of Celtic script. It's incredibly old."

Marcus shifted, his breath catching in anticipation. "And?"

Michael's pulse quickened as the meaning became clearer, the complexity of the words striking him. The inscription was a riddle, a veiled message shrouded in metaphors. His lips moved silently, repeating each phrase as it unraveled before him.

"'*Cenn naomh a chur suas, a shaol faoi bhréaga; éadrom mar ghaoth, ach ag déanamh cearta. Fuil rí na croí inár lámha.*'"

"'The saint raises his head, his life built on lies...'"

Lies? Michael translated slowly, verifying in his mind each interpretation, yet each word filling him with a creeping unease. His voice faltered. "'He is light as the wind but making what is right... and the blood of the king is in our hands.'"

The cryptic nature of the inscription gnawed at him, its phrasing too symbolic to be taken at face value. He knelt closer, his breath fogging the cold air as he continued reading.

"'The saint was not alone... the keys handed to Linus in shadow, and one lay claim to both...'" His eyes widened, the words settling like a stone in his chest. Some facts about Linus were foggy in history. It was acknowledged that Linus was the second bishop of Rome, after Peter, although the dates of his reign varied in *The Catholic Encyclopedia* from AD 64–76 or 67–79. He was credited with creating the first fifteen bishops and was a companion of Paul the Apostle. But these words implied that both he and Peter served the Church equally at the same time.

He whispered, "Peter wasn't the only one...."

Marcus leaned forward, his brows knitting. "What do you mean?"

"The inscription implies..." Michael swallowed hard, his mouth dry as the weight of the revelation sank in. "There was another. Linus, the second Bishop of Rome, who also held authority in the early Church, but their roles were concealed—deliberately hidden from the world. The power wasn't solely Peter's."

The silence stretched between them, thick with the implications. This was no mere historical footnote; it was a hidden truth, one that could undermine the origins of the Church itself.

"The inscription suggests that Peter's leadership wasn't absolute. Another, one named Linus, had the 'keys'—a symbol of authority." He hesitated, his mind racing. "If this were known..."

Marcus's face paled as realization dawned. "It would rewrite Church history."

Michael nodded, still staring at the sarcophagus. "The idea of Peter as the singular foundation of the Church, the first pope, the rock upon which everything was built... that belief holds everything together."

Marcus took a step back. "If people found out—"

"They won't," Michael said, though the words felt heavy on his tongue. "First, we don't know the author of this cryptic riddle, nor what authority or truth was behind those words. Too much needs to be researched before anyone can risk tearing apart centuries of faith and tradition."

All three stood in silence for a long moment, the catacombs pressing in around them, the air thick with history and secrets. Even here, beneath the holiest place in Christendom, the threat of conspiracy and the need for secrecy seemed to stir in the shadows.

Sofia finally spoke, her voice tight. "Do we tell anyone?"

Michael shook his head slowly. "Not yet, no. This inscription… it needs to be studied carefully. There's more here, I can feel it. But we need to proceed with caution. If certain people got wind of this—people with vested interests in preserving the Church's image—they could stop at nothing to bury it again. There will be those intent on keeping the Church free from the idea of a second person who could have been equally considered the first pope, a place we've reserved for St. Peter for centuries."

Marcus nodded grimly. "So, what do we do?"

"For now," Michael said, "we keep it between us. I'll dig deeper, try to understand the full meaning. But we can't let this information fall into the wrong hands."

The words lingered between them, and for the first time, Michael felt a chill that had nothing to do with the cold, subterranean air.

~

THE MID-AFTERNOON SUN filtered through the gauzy curtains of the small café, casting soft patches of gold across the polished table where Hana Sinclair and Elliot Voss sat. The murmur of conversation around them served as a muted backdrop to their exchange. A waiter discreetly placed a carafe of wine and two glasses between them, retreating with a bow.

Elliot leaned back in his chair, his posture effortlessly confident, as if the world and everyone in it were naturally inclined to bend to his will. His tailored gray suit, a sharp contrast to the rustic ambiance of the café, hinted at his polished, cosmopolitan edge.

"Thank you for meeting me, Hana," he began, his tone smooth and deliberate. His eyes, a piercing shade of blue, held hers for a beat longer than necessary. "Your reputation precedes you, of course. Le Monde's investigative star. But I have to say, I didn't expect you to agree so quickly."

Hana arched a brow, swirling the wine in her glass before taking a measured sip. "Curiosity, Mr. Voss. A journalist's most exploitable flaw."

"Elliot, please." He smiled, setting his own glass down without drinking. "And I'd say it's one of your most admirable qualities."

Hana offered a polite, practiced smile, one that revealed nothing. "Flattery aside, you mentioned wanting my thoughts on publicizing the bones exhibition. How could I refuse? It's not every day one gets to be part of history in the making."

Elliot leaned forward slightly, his fingers steepled. "Exactly. This isn't just an exhibition—it's a chance to reframe the Vatican's image for a modern audience. A narrative shift."

"An ambitious one," Hana replied. "The Church has a complicated history, to say the least. One exhibition won't undo centuries of controversy."

"True," Elliot conceded, his gaze intent. "But it's a start. And with the right touch, the right voice, it could spark something transformative. That's where you come in."

Hana tilted her head, her dark hair catching the sunlight in a way that seemed to distract him momentarily. "Me? I'm not sure what you're suggesting. *Le Monde* isn't exactly a public relations agency."

"No," he agreed, his voice low, almost intimate. "But you know how to tell a story, Hana. You know how to make people care. And you have an instinct for truth— one that people trust."

She set her glass down, watching him carefully. "Are you asking me to lend my byline to your project? Because that's not something I do."

"Not your byline," he said quickly, his tone shifting to something closer to entreaty. "Your insight. Your expertise. Just a few ideas to help shape the narrative, ensure it resonates. I wouldn't dream of compromising your integrity."

Hana studied him for a moment, letting the silence stretch. "If I did have ideas—and I'm not saying I do— they would involve authenticity. Transparency. People are skeptical of grand displays like this. It can't feel manufactured, or you'll lose them before you begin."

Elliot nodded, as though her words confirmed

something he already knew. "Exactly what I was hoping to hear. Tell me, how would you approach it? What story would you tell?"

Hana leaned back, crossing her legs deliberately. "Well, for starters, I'd focus on the human element. The history, the faith, the personal sacrifices made by those who safeguarded these relics. People connect with stories that feel personal, relatable."

"Beautifully said," Elliot murmured, his eyes not on her words but on her. "You have a way of making even the simplest truths sound profound."

Hana's lips curved, but she kept her tone light. "Is this your usual strategy, Mr.—Elliot? Showering people with compliments until they agree to help you?"

He chuckled, the sound low and warm. "Only when the compliments are genuine. You're… not what I expected, Hana."

She raised a brow. "And what did you expect?"

"Someone harder. Sharper. But there's an elegance to you, a subtlety." He smiled again, almost to himself. "It's disarming."

Hana's smile widened, though her eyes betrayed nothing. "Careful, Elliot. I might start to think you're using this publicity pitch as an excuse to flirt."

"Would you blame me if I were?" His words hung in the air between them, daring her to respond.

She held his gaze for a long moment before answering, her tone deliberately playful. "I'd say that would be a very inefficient use of your time."

Elliot chuckled again, raising his glass in a mock toast. "Efficiency is overrated."

They fell into a companionable silence, the charged undercurrent of their exchange still lingering.

Hana set her glass down and rose smoothly, her movements deliberate. "Thank you for the wine, Elliot. I'll think about your proposal and let you know if I have more thoughts."

He stood as well, his expression unreadable. "I'll look forward to it. And Hana... thank you. For your honesty."

She offered him a polite nod, her smile enigmatic. "It's the least I could do."

As she walked away, the sunlight catching her hair, Elliot watched her go, his expression thoughtful, a trace of a smile playing at his lips.

ELEVEN

The next day Elliot Voss sat in his darkened study, his fingers drumming lightly on the polished mahogany desk. The soft glow of a single lamp threw shadows across the room, making it feel like the walls themselves were conspiring with him. He glanced at the clock—time was running out. The public unveiling of St. Peter's bones was fast approaching, and the switch needed to be flawless. His fingers paused as he dialed Dr. Helena Barrett's number, the tension simmering beneath his calm exterior.

The phone rang once, twice, before Barrett picked up.

"Hello, Elliot," she greeted, her voice sharp and clinical. "I assume this isn't a social call."

He smirked. "You assume correctly, Helena. I need an update. How close are we to completing the replications?"

There was a pause. He could hear faint background

noise—maybe a lab environment, the hum of machinery, the clinking of instruments. Barrett's voice, though steady, carried an edge he hadn't noticed before.

"The process is... coming along," she replied, somewhat hesitantly. "I've used a combination of 3D scanning and printing, layering high-resolution scans of the original bones onto synthetic material that mimics the density and weight of first-century skeletal remains. I've also employed aging techniques—subtle discolorations, cracks, and even embedding ancient mineral traces into the bones. The fakes will be indistinguishable from the originals. At least, visually."

"And under scientific scrutiny?" Voss pressed, his voice low.

"I'm utilizing calcium hydroxylapatite, the mineral found in fossilized bones, in the replication. It holds up to most types of spectroscopic analysis, but... of course, if someone runs a full chemical assay, there's always a chance the truth will come out. But short of that, these bones will pass any physical examination."

Voss listened carefully, satisfied but sensing a hesitation in her tone that he couldn't ignore. Something was off.

"Dr. Barrett, what aren't you telling me?" he asked, his voice tightening.

She hesitated, and when she spoke again, her voice was strained, as if she were holding something back. "I've... I've had a visitor."

Voss straightened in his chair, his eyes narrowing. "A visitor?"

"Yes... Emilio Rossi," she finally confessed, her

words spilling out in a rush. "He showed up unannounced at my home lab. He made some... unsettling remarks. He seemed to figure out exactly what I was working on."

The name hit Voss like a jolt. Dr. Emilio Rossi—the renowned anthropologist at Sapienza University, had close ties to the Vatican. The last thing they needed was someone with Rossi's expertise sniffing around.

"How did he find out?" Voss growled.

"I don't know," Barrett replied, her voice betraying a growing panic. She wasn't about to tell him of the papers she had taken home for further study. "He must have made assumptions. He might have pieced things together. He's incredibly sharp. I tend to doubt he would, but if he digs any deeper, he could expose everything."

Voss leaned back in his chair, his mind racing. Rossi could be dangerous, not because of his position, but because of his intellect. He could unravel things if he so much as glimpsed the full picture, especially with the upcoming publicity of the exhibition.

"I assume you didn't confirm anything," Voss said, his tone icy.

"Of course not," Barrett snapped, though there was a tremor in her voice. "But he's no fool. He might know something is going on, and if he keeps pressing—"

"Leave him to me," Voss interrupted, his voice calm but laced with menace. "Rossi will be dealt with. You just focus on the bones. I don't care what it takes. Finish them. And don't breathe a word of this to anyone else. Understood?"

Barrett's voice was tight. "Understood."

Voss ended the call and sat in silence for a moment, his mind calculating the next move. Dr. Rossi was a liability now, one that couldn't be ignored.

He reached for another phone, this one secured. A different number, a different contact. As it rang, he stared out the window into the dark Roman night.

CHAPTER

TWELVE

D r. Simon Ginzberg stood at his office window
in the Caprioli Palace looking out over the
Teller University campus. Young people
congregated around the reflecting pool in the center of
the quad, many engaged in idle chatter, most hunched
over phones clutched in their hands as they sat on the
expansive lawn beneath Italian stone pines, their
distinctive flat, umbrella-shaped canopies spread wide
atop tall, slender trunks.

Typical days would normally find Simon in the
Vatican's Pius XII Reading Room, poring over ancient
manuscripts from the time of the Crusades, his
particular expertise, or more recently into the freshly
released correspondence and documents of Pope Pius
XII's reign.

The actions of Pius XII, born Eugenio Pacelli, during
World War II had been the subject of much debate and

controversy regarding his stance toward the Nazis. Some critics argued that the pope was too silent or passive in the face of the Holocaust, not speaking out forcefully enough against Nazi atrocities, particularly the persecution of Jews. They pointed to his reluctance to publicly condemn Adolf Hitler and the Nazi regime, and his diplomatic neutrality, as reasons for claiming that he didn't do enough to oppose Nazism.

However, defenders of Pius XII argued that behind the scenes, the pope worked to save thousands of Jews by instructing Catholic institutions, including monasteries and convents, to shelter Jews during the Holocaust. Additionally, they suggested that Pius maintained a cautious public stance to avoid provoking greater Nazi retaliation against Catholics and Jews, believing that diplomatic efforts and secret interventions would be more effective than public denunciations.

Simon's research into the papers of Pius XII was meant to help determine the pope's actual role during the war in as unbiased a treatment as possible.

The old scholar turned away from the window, his mind still churning with the implications of his latest findings. He walked to his desk, littered with photocopies of letters and wartime telegrams, each one a potential piece of the puzzle.

A sharp knock at the door startled him. "Come in," he called out, straightening his posture.

Elena Rossi, his research assistant, entered the office, her face flushed. "Dr. Ginzberg, my father is on the phone for you. He seems particularly focused on something and wants to see you today if your schedule permits."

"Really?" Simon mused, taking his seat and reaching for the phone. "Emilio, my old friend. To what do I owe this pleasure?"

"Good morning, Simon," the long-familiar voice said. "I trust I'm not interrupting your work? Have you got a few minutes?"

"Of course. What's on your mind?"

Emilio hesitated for a moment, choosing his words carefully. The connection crackled faintly, but Simon could still hear the tension in his old friend's voice.

"There's something… odd I've stumbled upon. I'm not sure how to describe it, and frankly, I don't want to get into it over the phone. It's sensitive."

Simon leaned forward, his curiosity piqued. Emilio Rossi wasn't one for dramatics, and if he was being this cautious, it had to be something significant. "Odd? You've got me intrigued already. What sort of 'something' are we talking about?"

"It concerns Dr. Helena Barrett," Emilio said, his tone lowering, as if the mere mention of her name carried weight. "You know she's been involved in some high-level projects lately, don't you?"

"Yes, I've heard whispers," Simon replied, frowning. "Barrett's been working on archaeological replicas, hasn't she? But nothing too controversial from what I've gathered."

"That's just the surface," Emilio muttered. "Look, Simon, what I'm about to say could have serious implications for the Vatican… and for both of us if this gets out prematurely. I believe she's involved in something much bigger than simple replicas. It looks like she's—" He paused, taking a deep breath. "She might be replicating old bones, Simon. Bones of great interest to the Vatican. And I'm not talking about just any bones."

Simon's mind immediately raced to the possibilities. "Replicating bones? You mean… relics?"

"That's what I'm starting to suspect," Emilio replied grimly. "I can't say for sure, but there are too many coincidences, and she was nervous, even secretive, when I asked. I've seen her with references to materials and scans that align with something I recently came across in the Vatican Archives."

He added, his voice tense but determined. "I don't want to risk putting the details in writing or over the phone. I mean, it could be nothing. And if this gets out before I have a chance to verify everything, it could turn into a disaster."

"Fair enough," Simon agreed. "Are you thinking of coming to see me? I'm at the university for most of the day."

"That's exactly what I was hoping," Emilio said with a sigh of relief. "I'll drive out to Zagarolo. I can be there in about an hour and a half. There's more I need to tell you, things that I can't explain until we're face to face."

Simon nodded, though Emilio couldn't see him. "I'll be here. I'll make sure we've got privacy. You can explain everything when you get here."

"Thank you, Simon," Emilio said, his voice softening. "I'll leave now and be there soon."

"Drive safely," Simon said, his mind already turning over the implications of what Emilio might reveal. As the call ended, he remained seated, again staring out the window of his small office. Something stirred in the pit of his stomach, a quiet but insistent feeling of unease.

THIRTEEN

Emilio Rossi guided his car along the quiet country road, leaving the bustling streets of Rome behind. The sun cast a soft amber glow over the rolling hills of Lazio. It was a peaceful drive, the kind that allowed his mind to drift, to chew on the puzzle that had been gnawing at him for days. His discovery back at Barrett's lab had set off alarm bells in his mind. Why would Helena, of all people, be so secretive? Everyone knew she was an expert at replicating artifacts for public displays and private collections. So why had she been so defensive when he had asked her about her recent work?

Teller University was just over an hour away, perched in the sleepy town of Zagarolo. Rossi gripped the wheel a little tighter, the growing feeling of unease creeping into his thoughts. *It was nothing*, he told himself. Just the nerves that came with chasing down a mystery this curious and potentially important.

As the road began to climb into the hills outside the city, the landscape shifted from sprawling farmlands to steep, winding curves that cut through thick patches of trees. Rossi was used to these roads—he had driven them countless times on his way to the university. He downshifted as he began the familiar descent on the other side, the car picking up speed as the grade steepened.

But then, something felt off.

His foot pressed lightly on the brake, expecting the usual resistance, but the pedal sank to the floor with a sickening ease. No response. He pressed again, harder this time, but the car didn't slow. Instead, it accelerated, the engine purring with menace as the decline grew steeper.

Rossi's heart skipped a beat. He glanced at the dashboard—no warning lights, no sign of malfunction. His mind raced, searching for a rational explanation, but there was none. The brakes were simply gone.

The car was moving faster now, the curves of the road coming quicker, sharper. He gripped the wheel with both hands, knuckles white, and tried to downshift again, praying the engine would slow the vehicle. It barely made a difference. The car groaned as it resisted, but the momentum was too great.

Panic clawed at him. The trees blurred as he hurtled down the road, the narrow lanes offering no room for error. His pulse pounded in his ears, a steady rhythm of terror as the car careened around a bend, tires skidding dangerously close to the edge of the road. One wrong move, and he would plunge into the ravine below.

"Come on, come on!" Rossi muttered to himself, frantically pumping the brake pedal as if sheer will could force it to work. He yanked the emergency brake, but it too gave nothing but a feeble jolt, barely slowing the car. He was out of options.

Ahead, the road twisted sharply, and beyond that— the glint of metal. A truck! A semi-truck, crawling along the slope in the opposite lane, its massive bulk blocking most of the road. Rossi's stomach dropped.

The car hurtled forward, closing the distance faster than he could process. There was no space to pass, no shoulder to veer onto. His mind screamed at him to do something, anything, but the wheel felt useless in his hands.

The semi's headlights loomed larger, its horn blaring a warning that reverberated through his bones. Rossi swerved hard to the right, tires screeching as the car spun, the world tilting on its axis. Time seemed to slow, the sounds of the road falling away into a surreal silence, save for the frantic pounding of his own heart.

In that final, agonizing moment, Rossi saw the driver's face—a look of horror mirrored in his own.

Then—impact.

Metal crunched against metal, the force of the collision wrenching Rossi's body forward as the car slammed into the side of the semi. The sound was deafening, a sickening mix of shattering glass, bending steel, and the violent thud of the crash. The front of his car crumpled like paper, the momentum carrying it under the semi's trailer before coming to a brutal, grinding halt.

For a moment, everything was still.

The smell of gasoline filled the air, mingling with the acrid stench of burnt rubber. Smoke rose in thick plumes from the wreckage. Inside the twisted remains of his car, Emilio Rossi lay motionless, his lifeless body trapped in the mangled ruins.

FAR AWAY, in the quiet of his own office, Elliot Voss received a call. He listened to the report dispassionately.

Rossi wouldn't be a problem anymore.

FOURTEEN

The late afternoon sun formed long shadows over the quiet street where Elena Rossi lived, her small apartment tucked away in a leafy corner of Zagarolo. She had left the office early and now sat at the kitchen table, lost in her work, when the phone rang—its shrill tone cutting through the stillness of the room. She glanced at the screen, unfamiliar with the number but picking up instinctively.

"*Pronto*?" she answered.

"Signora Elena Rossi?" a deep, formal voice responded.

"Yes, speaking."

"This is Colonel Carlo Bianchi of the Carabinieri," he said, his tone steady but carrying the weight of years in law enforcement. "I'm afraid I have some difficult news."

Elena's heart skipped a beat. Her breath caught as

she gripped the phone tighter. "What is it? What happened?"

Bianchi hesitated, just for a moment, before continuing. "I regret to inform you that your father, Dr. Emilio Rossi, was involved in a fatal accident earlier today. His car crashed on the road to Zagarolo. I'm so sorry for your loss."

The words hit her like a punch to the chest, driving the air from her lungs. "No..." Elena whispered, disbelief flooding her voice. "That can't be true. My father... he was just on his way to meet someone. He can't be—"

"We've confirmed it, Signora Rossi," Bianchi said softly. "His vehicle collided with a semi-truck after what appears to have been a brake failure on a steep descent."

Elena went silent, her hand shaking as she pressed the phone to her ear, struggling to process the words. It felt surreal, distant—like some terrible dream she would wake up from.

After a beat, Bianchi's voice returned, calm but deliberate. "I do have to ask you a few questions, Signora. I know this is a terrible time, but... was your father in any trouble? Did he have any enemies that you're aware of?"

"Enemies?" she repeated, her mind reeling. "No, of course not. My father was a respected scholar. Why would anyone...?"

Bianchi shifted slightly, lowering his voice, though Elena couldn't see the troubled look crossing his face. "We're still investigating the cause of the crash. At first glance, it seems like a mechanical failure—a brake malfunction—but there are… some anomalies that we're looking into."

Elena's head spun as she struggled to understand. "Anomalies? What do you mean?"

"The brakes appear to have been tampered with," Bianchi said cautiously, avoiding technical details but implying enough for the suspicion to hang in the air. "We found signs that the brake lines were damaged, possibly before the crash. But nothing's confirmed yet. We're trying to rule out foul play."

"Foul play?" Elena echoed, her voice cracking under the strain of it all. "You're saying someone might have… done this to him?"

"It's just a line of inquiry we're pursuing," Bianchi replied gently but firmly. "I didn't want to alarm you, but it's important we understand if your father had any reason to be a target. Had he mentioned anyone troubling him recently? Anything that stood out?"

Elena swallowed hard, her throat tight. "No… nothing like that. My father didn't have enemies. He was just going about his work. He never mentioned feeling threatened." Her voice wavered as she spoke, the reality beginning to settle like a weight pressing down on her chest.

"I see," Bianchi said, his tone thoughtful. "We'll continue our investigation, and I'll keep you informed as we know more. Again, I'm very sorry for your loss."

Elena barely mumbled her thanks, numb with grief and confusion as she hung up the phone. The words hung in the air—"foul play," "brake failure," "enemies." None of it made sense. Her father was a man of history, not a man who courted danger. How could this have happened?

She sat in silence for a long time, the walls of the apartment feeling like they were closing in on her, until finally, she reached for her phone again. Her fingers trembled as she dialed the number for Simon Ginzberg, her father's closest colleague and a man she had known since childhood.

"Simon," she said when he picked up, her voice small and broken.

"Elena?" Simon's voice came through, concerned. "What's the matter?"

"It's my father…" Elena began, and then the words broke free in a rush, her voice cracking as she continued, "He's dead. He was in a car accident on his way to see you… and they think it wasn't an accident."

There was a pause on the other end of the line, the silence heavy and disbelieving.

"Elena…" Simon's voice was soft, pained. "I—I don't know what to say. I'm so sorry. What happened?"

"They think someone might have tampered with his brakes," she said, barely holding back a sob. "They asked me if he had enemies. Enemies, Simon! I don't understand. He didn't… he couldn't have…"

Her voice broke completely now, and she began to cry, the grief overwhelming her. Simon's heart twisted at the sound of it. He had known Emilio for years, worked alongside him, respected him deeply. The news struck him hard, like a blow to the chest.

"Elena, I'm so sorry," he whispered. "I can't believe this. I don't know what to say, but I'm here. I'll help you in any way I can. We'll find out what happened, I promise."

But Elena was barely listening now, the sobs racking her body as the enormity of her loss washed over her.

Simon remained on the line, his own mind racing, already trying to piece together the last conversations he'd had with Emilio, wondering if what Emilio had wanted to talk to him about could possibly fit into this horrid reality.

Nothing made sense right now to Simon, and only one thing was clear: Emilio was gone.

FIFTEEN

Father Michael sat alone in his study, the light of his desk lamp reflecting off the walls around him. His notes lay before him, but the words from the catacombs echoed in his mind with a force he could hardly contain.

"Linus, the alternate rock upon which the Church shall stand."

His fingers trembled as he ran them across the page. The inscription—written in the ancient, forgotten Brythonic script—kept repeating in his head, louder and louder with each passing hour. Linus... not merely St. Peter's successor, but his equal, no one "true rock"? Linus, as well as Peter, the man whose legacy was singular and unquestioned? It was almost too much to absorb.

Michael leaned back in his chair, staring blankly at the crucifix on the wall. For centuries, Peter had been regarded as the sole *rock* upon which Christ had declared He would build His Church. The "keeper of the keys," the central figure in the unbroken apostolic succession that had led to the current papacy itself. But this new revelation—this hidden truth from the catacombs—suggested something far more disturbing.

"Peter was not alone," Michael muttered under his breath, his voice barely audible. He stood and paced the room, the pull of the past pressing down on him.

How could this be? If Linus had been anointed as an equal rock, it would fundamentally alter the way the Church had understood its foundation for millennia. The very nature of the papacy, the unchallenged spiritual authority derived from Peter as the first pope, would suddenly seem more complicated, less singular. Linus had always been recognized as Peter's successor, the second Bishop of Rome, but this inscription suggested he was more than that. A *co-equal* guardian of the Church's beginnings. What if Peter hadn't been alone in holding the keys to the kingdom?

If Linus had shared that role, had Christ's words to Peter—"*Upon this rock, I will build my Church*"—been misunderstood? Or had those words been deliberately misinterpreted by those who sought to elevate Peter above all others?

Michael stopped, staring at the floor as if the answers might materialize in the woodgrain. The Church, in its ancient tradition, had maintained Peter as the singular foundation, the conduit between Christ's authority and the earthly institution of the papacy. To suggest that Peter hadn't stood alone, that another had been chosen with equal standing, could destabilize everything.

It could mean that the Church had always been meant to be a more collaborative institution, its leadership not concentrated in a single figurehead but shared among a sacred few.

The inferences would shake the very basis of the Church's tradition of papal supremacy. For nearly two millennia, the Church had been built upon the idea of apostolic succession, the singularity of Peter's authority passed down through the centuries from one pope to the next. *One rock. One holder of the keys.* But this discovery implied dual authority, or perhaps a council of apostles intended to lead the Church—a dynamic completely at odds with the centralized papal tradition.

He could already hear the voices in his head— cardinals, theologians, devout believers—crying heresy at the mere suggestion. The Church's legitimacy, the infallibility of papal decrees, the very essence of its spiritual power rested on Peter's unique place in history. If Linus had been entrusted with the same authority, had the Church unknowingly or purposefully suppressed that truth?

Michael's thoughts drifted to the present-day Vatican. How would the hierarchy react to such a discovery? There were men in Rome who would do anything to keep this buried—men who valued tradition over truth, who would stop at nothing to protect the Church from scandal. The implications weren't just theological; they were political. Such a truth could shatter centuries of established order.

"Two rocks... not one," he whispered, pacing again. "If Linus was an equal foundation, the entire history of the Church's development needs to be reexamined. All those centuries of succession, of Peter's singular authority... it would mean we've been following a half-truth."

Michael's mind raced with the implications for modern doctrine. Could this explain the longstanding schisms in the Church? The power struggles, the corruption, the fractures that had emerged over time? Had the Church strayed from its true path, failing to recognize that Peter's authority had been shared from the beginning? What if the very division within the Church—Orthodox and Catholic, reformist and conservative—stemmed from a fundamental misunderstanding of its foundation? Could two or more acting as the Church's foundational authority—maybe even a council—have avoided the turmoil that the Church had suffered at various times?

And then there was the question of why this had been hidden for so long. The inscription had been carved in secret, deep in the catacombs, as if those who knew the truth had been forced to bury it. Was it fear of persecution? Fear of what this knowledge would do to the fragile post-revolutionary Church? Or had there been deliberate suppression by those in power, afraid of what it would mean to acknowledge another "rock" besides Peter?

Michael sank into his chair, his head in his hands. The responsibility of this knowledge weighed heavily on him. What was he supposed to do with this revelation? Could he even dare to share it, knowing the potential fallout? The Church had faced crises before, but this—this could fracture it at its core.

His mind wandered back to the inscription: *Linus, the alternate rock upon which the Church shall stand.* If Peter had passed not only his mantle but his spiritual authority to Linus, then the Church had been built on a dual foundation. But the world had never known it. How different might the Church's history have been if Linus had been recognized as Peter's equal? Would it have led to a more balanced leadership, one that resisted the concentration of power, or would it have torn the fledgling religion apart?

Michael's heart pounded in his chest. He knew the discovery was explosive, but he also knew the truth couldn't remain hidden forever. And yet, exposing it could ignite a firestorm. Was he ready for that? Was anyone?

With a deep sigh, Michael closed his eyes and prayed for guidance. The Church had always been about faith, not just in God, but in the truth. And truth, however painful, had a way of revealing itself in time.

Opening his eyes again, he resolved to proceed carefully. If this knowledge was going to come to light, it would have to be done with care—slowly, methodically. But he knew one thing for certain: the Church, as it stood today, would never be the same once this secret was known.

SIXTEEN

T he trattoria was tucked away on a narrow street near the Piazza Navona, one of those Roman gems with worn wooden tables and a sun-bleached awning flapping gently in the breeze. It was quiet, save for the occasional clatter of dishes from the back kitchen and the muted hum of distant conversations. A carafe of red wine sat between them, untouched, though both had glasses in hand. Michael's expression was clouded, his brow furrowed as he glanced over at Hana, who was slicing through her plate of pasta with mechanical precision, as if her mind was elsewhere.

"You can't be serious, Hana," Michael said, his voice low, but with an edge of disbelief.

Hana sighed and set her fork down, looking at him with that intense gaze of hers that always seemed to pierce whatever noise surrounded them. "I am serious,

Michael. You can't tell anyone. Not about this. Not now."

"You're telling me to keep the discovery of Linus a secret? You understand the magnitude of this, don't you?" His eyes flickered with frustration, his fingers tapping against the side of his wine glass. "This changes everything. History, theology, even the Church's identity. The Vatican—"

"The Vatican will do what it always does," Hana interrupted, leaning forward slightly. "It'll control the narrative. Think about it. If you reveal this now, the Church will either bury it to protect itself, or they'll exploit it to their advantage, twisting the significance to fit their agenda. And where does that leave you? They'll use you, Michael."

He shook his head, leaning back in his chair as if to distance himself from her words. "It's not about me, Hana. This is bigger than all of us. The truth—"

"The truth will get you crucified," Hana said softly, her tone almost sad as she looked away for a moment, out to the cobblestone street where a couple strolled by, oblivious to the weight of their conversation. She turned back to him, eyes sharp again. "Think about the timing. The bones of St. Peter are about to go on display, an unprecedented event. If you come out with this now, the Church will be in chaos. They won't know how to handle it."

"I don't want to hide this, Hana. I can't just sit on something this important." His voice had lowered again, the intensity in his words undercut by a weariness, a tension that had been tightening inside him since the moment he had uncovered the truth. "What if it leaks? Someone else will find out eventually."

"And that's exactly why you should wait." Hana's hands rested flat on the table now, as if trying to steady them. "You have control right now. You know the truth, and no one else does. If you release this information, you lose that control, and I guarantee you won't like what happens next."

Michael stared at her, his eyes flicking down to the table, then back up again. "What if it's wrong? What if I misinterpreted the data? I... I've checked everything a dozen times, but what if I'm wrong?"

Hana leaned back in her chair, her eyes softening slightly. "You're not wrong. You wouldn't have brought it up if you weren't absolutely sure."

He let out a breath, one hand dragging through his hair. "Then what do I do? Sit on it forever? Watch the Church move forward with St. Peter's bones while knowing that Linus, an actual co-pope, is buried beneath our feet and forgotten? This would change the very basis of the papacy and its apostolic succession."

"I'm not saying wait forever," Hana replied, her voice gentler now, as though sensing how close he was to the edge. "But right now... think about the stakes. The Church, the faithful, the world—they're not ready for this. And you're not ready for the consequences."

Michael was silent for a long moment, his eyes distant as he stared down at the red wine swirling in his glass. He couldn't shake the weight of the discovery. The Church's legacy was built on centuries of reverence for St. Peter, and now... this.

Hana considered him for a moment, her expression unreadable, before she picked up her glass and took a small sip of wine. She set it down slowly, then met his eyes. "Keep it quiet, at least for now. Use the time to figure out the bigger picture. Look at who gains from this and who loses. You need to know what kind of battle you're about to start before you draw your sword."

Michael let her words settle, the tension in his shoulders easing just slightly. He knew she was right, even if he didn't want to admit it. The revelation was too volatile, too massive to simply thrust into the light without considering the repercussions.

He sighed, finally taking a sip of his own wine. "You make it sound so simple."

"It's not simple," Hana said with a faint, almost bitter smile. "Nothing ever is. But sometimes... the truth has to wait."

"What about Elliot Voss?" Michael asked suddenly, his voice low but edged with tension. "He's been... too involved. Snooping around places he has no business being."

Hana shifted in her seat, her expression tightening. She glanced around briefly to ensure no one was paying attention before responding. "Voss is opportunistic, yes," she admitted, her tone guarded. "But he's not a threat—not to you. We met for drinks the other night, by the way."

Michael raised an eyebrow, his gaze piercing. "You had drinks with him?"

Hana's lips curved into a faint smile, though it didn't

quite reach her eyes. "To discuss publicity for the exhibition, Michael. He wanted my perspective on how to frame the event for maximum impact. I listened, I gave him a few harmless suggestions, and I left. That's all."

His jaw tightened. "Hana, he's not just some slick businessman. He's got an agenda. And you're…" He paused, searching for the right words. "You're clever, but Voss plays a long game. He doesn't make a move unless he sees a way to benefit."

"Then it's a good thing I'm not easily swayed," she replied, her voice steady, almost teasing. She leaned forward slightly, her expression softening. "Michael, I know how to handle men like Voss. Trust me. He's curious about me, sure. Maybe even a little intrigued." She gave a sly smile. "But I'm not letting him get close to anything that matters."

Michael frowned, his fingers tapping an uneven rhythm on the edge of the table. "You think you can control him?"

"I *know* I can," Hana said firmly, her confidence unwavering. "He's trying to charm me into playing along, and I'm letting him think it's working. That's all."

Michael exhaled slowly, but the knot of unease in his chest only tightened. "He's dangerous, Hana. More dangerous than you realize. I've seen men like him— masters at twisting situations to their advantage. And I can't shake the feeling he's already too close to something we're not seeing."

Hana's gaze softened, a flicker of understanding passing between them. "I get it. You're worried. And maybe you're right to be. But I'm not some naïve rookie, Michael. I can keep Voss at arm's length while figuring out what he's really after."

Michael met her eyes, searching for reassurance. Her confidence was steady, but it didn't fully ease his concern. He leaned back in his chair, his mind turning over possibilities. "Just... don't underestimate him. Or let him get under your skin."

"Noted." Hana gave him a small, reassuring smile, though her eyes betrayed a hint of worry. "But you need to focus on your own moves, Michael. Once you start pulling at these threads, there's no telling how fast or how far everything unravels."

He nodded slowly, her words weighing heavily. "I know," he said quietly. "And that's what scares me."

For a moment, silence stretched between them again, the air thick with unspoken fears. Michael looked at her, knowing she could hold her own but still feeling the pang of jealousy he couldn't quite suppress. Voss was circling too close, and Hana's proximity to the man only added to his unease.

"Be careful, Hana," he said finally.

Her smile returned, softer this time, almost tender. "Always."

But as she sipped her wine, Michael's mind raced. If Voss was indeed circling, then it wasn't just Hana he had to protect—it was everything. And the walls felt like they were closing in faster than ever.

CHAPTER
SEVENTEEN

Marcus Russo sat at his cluttered desk, the soft hum of the Vatican office building a strange comfort amid his growing sense of unease. Papers and excavation reports lay in organized disarray, reminders of a career steeped in meticulous research, his life's work cataloging and safeguarding the Church's ancient treasures. Yet today, none of that mattered. He was consumed by one thing: the inscription.

Michael's interpretation of the Linus inscription had struck him like a lightning bolt, shattering the comfortable narrative he had always taken for granted —Peter, the unchallenged first pope, the rock upon which Christ had built His Church. But now... Linus? The name lingered in his mind, gnawing at him with its implications. He ran a hand through his thinning hair, his fingers brushing over the stubble that lined his jaw. The weight of it all pressed down on him. It wasn't the discovery itself that disturbed him, but what it represented.

Marcus was, by nature, a pragmatist. He had spent his entire career unraveling historical puzzles, piecing together fragments of forgotten lives from ancient artifacts and inscriptions. His work wasn't about glory or public recognition; it was about truth. The truth buried beneath centuries of dust and dogma, waiting to be uncovered. The past, to him, wasn't a relic to be revered but a living, breathing thing—a mirror to the present. And now, that mirror was reflecting something deeply unsettling.

He leaned back in his chair, staring up at the frescoed ceiling. Was Linus truly Peter's equal, or even his superior, in those early years? Could the Church have been built on a foundation other than Peter's? The implications were seismic. He knew, better than most, how the early Church had been a chaotic, fluid institution, full of competing ideas, rival sects, and theological debates. It wasn't hard to imagine a scenario in which Peter's primacy had been... negotiated, or even contested.

But that's not what bothered him. What gnawed at his soul was the idea that *this*—this discovery, this potential rewriting of history—could challenge the very structure of the Church today. If Peter's primacy were ever seriously questioned, what would that mean for everything the Church stood for? Would believers lose faith in the institution that had been their spiritual guide for two millennia? Would the hierarchy crumble?

Marcus rubbed his temples, feeling the familiar pulse

of a headache coming on. His mind swirled with questions, each one pulling him deeper into the labyrinth of possibilities. He thought of his years as a young archaeologist, just starting out, full of hope and ambition. He had dreamed of finding something— something that would change the world. But now, with the weight of this discovery pressing on him, he wasn't sure he wanted to be the one to unlock this particular door.

He glanced over at the thick, worn volumes of early Church history that lined the shelves of his office. One, in particular, caught his eye: *Eusebius's Ecclesiastical History*. He had read it a hundred times, using it as a roadmap to navigate the often murky waters of early Christian traditions. And yet, now, it seemed so incomplete, so... sanitized. What had been left out? What had been rewritten? Was Linus nothing more than a footnote because it was convenient for him to be?

As the questions circled in his mind, Marcus felt a cold weight settle in his chest. *What do I do with this?* He wasn't naive. He knew that history was often written by those in power and that the Church had always been protective of its narrative, particularly when it came to its origins. Revealing this now—at a time when faith and authority were already being tested—would be more than controversial. It could be catastrophic.

He picked up the piece of paper on which he had scribbled Michael's interpretation of the inscription. "Peter-Linus." Two names, side by side. Equals? Successors? Rivals? He didn't know yet. But he knew one thing: this wasn't going away. The inscription was real, and so were its implications. Marcus was a man who sought the truth, no matter where it led. He couldn't simply walk away from this, nor could he sit quietly and let others decide what it meant.

But how far was he willing to go? He had a family. A wife. Children. A life of comfort that he had built within the walls of the Vatican. Was it worth risking all of that to chase the truth? Would anyone even listen? Or worse —would they try to silence him?

His pulse quickened as he considered the possibilities. If he kept this quiet, he could continue his work as before, his life undisturbed. But if he pursued it... if he let this discovery out into the world... the consequences could be beyond anything he had ever imagined.

And then, like a whisper from the back of his mind, a thought began to take shape. *What if Linus wasn't just a footnote? What if his role had been deliberately minimized?* Marcus's professional instinct told him there was more to uncover. More inscriptions, more clues, hidden in plain sight. The puzzle wasn't complete yet, and he needed to see it through.

Suddenly, his decision was clear. He would investigate. Quietly. Discreetly. He would follow the trail of Linus wherever it led, but he wouldn't be reckless. He would gather evidence, carefully and methodically, before making any decisions about what to do next. If there was something more to this story, he would find it. But he would do it on his terms.

Marcus rose from his chair and crossed the room to his bookshelf. He pulled down *Eusebius* and began flipping through the pages, searching for references to Linus. The book felt heavier in his hands than usual, as though the voice of antiquity itself was pressing down on him.

"Linus, Linus, Linus," he muttered to himself as his fingers danced across the pages.

Whatever the truth was, he knew one thing for certain: it was going to change everything. And there was no turning back now.

But what if, in uncovering the truth, he discovered something the world wasn't ready to hear?

He sat back down, the weight of the unknown pressing in around him. Marcus Russo, the Vatican's faithful archaeologist, had become the keeper of a secret that could shake the foundations of faith itself. And for the first time in his life, he wasn't sure if he was ready for the consequences.

CHAPTER
EIGHTEEN

S imon Ginzberg sat in his office, staring at the darkened screen of his phone, his mind still buzzing with the words Emilio had said yesterday morning. It hadn't been a long call, but it had been enough to plant a seed of worry in Simon's mind, a worry that had grown steadily throughout the day. And now, with Emilio dead, the worry had bloomed into full-blown suspicion.

The accident had been sudden—brake failure, they said. A tragic incident on the country road to Zagarolo. But Simon couldn't shake the uneasy feeling gnawing at his gut. Especially not after their conversation the day before. And Emilio's daughter explaining the police were considering foul play.

He could still hear Emilio's voice, low and tense, as if he were afraid someone might be listening. *"I believe she's involved in something much bigger than simple replicas.*

It looks like she's—she might be replicating old bones, Simon. Bones of great interest to the Vatican. And I'm not talking about just any bones..."

Simon had been confused at first, unsure of the significance. *"Replicating bones? You mean... relics?"*

Emilio had paused, as if weighing his words carefully. *"I don't want to risk putting the details in writing or over the phone... There's more I need to tell you, things that I can't explain until we're face to face."*

But Emilio never got the chance. An hour later, he was dead, and Simon was left with a growing sense of unease and far too many questions. *Replicating bones... whose bones?* Emilio had never said. He hadn't had the chance.

Simon leaned back in his chair, running a hand through his clipped Van Dyke, trying to make sense of it all. Barrett was a known expert in her field, a specialist in relics and antiquities, but forgeries? That wasn't her usual territory. And what was she planning to do with these replicas? The question had gnawed at him ever since the phone call, and now, in the quiet of his office, Simon's mind began to turn over the possibilities.

Whose bones could be so important?

He stood and began pacing, thinking aloud to the empty room. "She's not just doing this for academic purposes. Emilio said these aren't just any bones. They must have significant value... historically, religiously."

Then, like a flash of lightning, the thought hit him. *St. Peter's Bones Exhibition!* The Vatican was about to unveil one of its most sacred relics—the bones of St.

Peter, the first pope, the rock upon which the Church itself had been built. Could it be? Was Barrett involved in replicating *those* bones?

The idea seemed impossible at first, absurd even. The Vatican's security surrounding such a sacred event was beyond meticulous. The bones had been under scrutiny for decades, their authenticity beyond question. But the more Simon thought about it, the more the pieces began to fit.

What if Barrett was replicating St. Peter's bones? It made a twisted kind of sense. If someone had access to perfect replicas of the bones, they could swap them out, display the forgeries to the world, and no one would be the wiser. And most likely there were numerous more opportunities to do that when the bones went on public display. But why? What would be the point?

Simon frowned, trying to follow the thread. What good would having the authentic bones do anyone beyond the ego of having procured them? That was enough motivation for some, surely, but Simon realized it wasn't about ego but more likely about money—at least, not in the traditional sense. This would likely be bigger than just the loss of an authentic artifact. The Vatican itself was the target. Undermining the authenticity of St. Peter's bones would be an attack on the Church's credibility, its authority. The ramifications would be enormous. A scandal of that magnitude could shake the very core of Catholicism.

The thought sent a chill through Simon's spine. Was that the plan? Was someone trying to destabilize the

Church, using Barrett's expertise to orchestrate the perfect crime?

He stopped pacing, his mind racing. He couldn't prove any of this, of course. It was all speculation. But the pieces were starting to align, and the possibility that Emilio's death wasn't just an accident was becoming harder to ignore. If Emilio had uncovered part of this conspiracy—if he had gotten too close to the truth—then it made sense why he had been silenced.

Simon felt a tightening in his chest, a mix of anger and fear. He couldn't sit on this any longer. Emilio could have told someone of his contact with Simon and his reason for that drive. They might assume that Simon, too, was privy to what might be going on. Emilio had died trying to expose something, and if Simon didn't act, he might be the next target. He needed answers, and only one person he knew could help him navigate this—Father Michael Dominic.

Michael had the connections, the insight, and the moral compass to see this through. He was also the one person Simon knew could be trusted within the Vatican's inner circles. If something were happening with the bones, Michael could find out. And more importantly, he would be able to keep them both from getting killed in the process.

Simon grabbed his coat and keys, moving quickly toward the door. There wasn't a moment to waste. He had to get to Michael, and they had to figure this out—before anyone else ended up like Emilio.

As he stepped into the cool morning air, Simon

couldn't shake the feeling that he was walking into something much bigger than he could handle alone. But there was no turning back now. The truth, whatever it was, had to come out. And Simon would make sure that Emilio's death wasn't in vain.

NINETEEN

Early that morning, the Vatican's ornate halls echoed with the hushed tones of preparation. The upcoming exhibition of St. Peter's bones was a monumental event—a rare chance for the public to glimpse one of Christianity's most sacred relics. In the main conference room, behind the heavy oak doors adorned with centuries-old carvings, the small committee overseeing the exhibition was gathered. At the head of the long table, Father Michael Dominic sat beside Monsignor Matteo Ferrante, who, as the coordinator of the event, had a watchful eye over every detail.

Across from them sat Elliot Voss, calm and composed, his fingers casually resting on the polished surface of the table. Papers and documents lay in front of him—event schedules, promotional materials, and meticulous timelines. His demeanor was relaxed, as if he were merely an observer in the process, yet every now and then, his gaze sharpened with the intensity of a man quietly pulling strings behind the scenes.

Ferrante motioned to Voss to explain his efforts in their plans.

"So," Voss began, his voice smooth and calm, "I've spoken to a few key people in the media and diplomatic spheres. The coverage for this exhibition is going to be unprecedented. We've secured interviews, feature articles, and even a few televised specials that will highlight the significance of this event not just for the Church, but for cultural and historical preservation."

Matteo, who had harbored some initial concerns about Voss's involvement, glanced at Father Michael and saw a flicker of approval in his colleague's eyes. Voss wasn't meddling, not yet. Instead, he appeared to be a facilitator, skillfully navigating the political and logistical challenges of organizing an event of this magnitude.

"This is more than I expected," Matteo admitted, leaning back in his chair. "The attention alone will draw thousands of pilgrims and tourists. I hadn't thought of bringing in the diplomatic circles, but it makes sense."

"We've secured prime coverage across multiple international outlets," Voss continued, his voice smooth and reassuring. "CNN, BBC, *Le Monde*—all the major networks. We'll have live broadcasts from the moment the doors open. Social media is already buzzing, and we've arranged exclusive interviews with key Church historians who will highlight the significance of the bones. This event will be global in scale."

Michael leaned forward in his seat, studying the documents that Voss had laid out. He had his reservations about the man, but there was no denying Voss's skill in orchestrating media. What would have taken the Vatican weeks of negotiation had been accomplished in a matter of days, and with startling efficiency.

"I have to admit," Father Michael said, a hint of admiration in his voice, "this is impressive. The kind of reach we'll have... it's unparalleled."

"Agreed," Ferrante chimed in, his tone more guarded but nonetheless approving. He was a man of the old guard, cautious and traditional, and had initially balked at Voss's involvement. But now, with the exhibition nearing, he couldn't deny the results. "The publicity alone will draw more attention to the spiritual significance of the relics. It seems your network is indeed well connected, Mr. Voss."

Voss met his gaze with cool assurance. "Absolutely. My team is already working with international outlets, coordinating security details with local law enforcement, and negotiating with sponsors who wish to support the event. All of this has been set in motion without burdening the Vatican with too much operational involvement. Consider this a partnership where your vision and my resources align perfectly."

Father Michael smiled at this. Voss's influence was palpable but not overbearing. The delicate balance between allowing him some control without compromising the sanctity of the event seemed, for now, to be holding. Voss was proving to be an asset, one that both Michael and Matteo had no choice but to appreciate, at least in these early stages.

Voss offered a polite smile, the kind that never quite reached his eyes. "I'm glad to hear that my efforts are appreciated, gentlemen. My goal has always been to ensure the success of this exhibition—to allow the world to see and understand the importance of the Vatican's treasures."

His words were smooth, well-rehearsed. There was nothing overtly disingenuous in his tone, yet Michael sensed a carefully calculated neutrality in Voss's manner. He never pushed too far, never made a suggestion that was beyond his modest purview as the exhibition's logistical consultant. He knew just how much to offer without appearing as if he were asserting control. It was masterful, in its own way.

Matteo Ferrante, however, was less attuned to the nuances of Voss's game. For him, the results were all that mattered. The logistics of the exhibition—security, scheduling, media relations—were all running smoothly, with far fewer complications than he had expected. His wrinkled brow, perpetually furrowed with concern, had eased somewhat in recent days.

"I have to say," Ferrante continued, leaning forward with a more earnest expression, "your team has been quite effective. Even with the heightened security, everything is ahead of schedule. The viewing platforms are being constructed on time, the VIP invitations have gone out without a hitch, and the media response has been enthusiastic, to say the least."

Michael watched Voss carefully. There it was again—

that flicker of something beneath his eyes, a subtle satisfaction that he quickly masked with a professional smile.

"We have a tight schedule to keep, of course," Voss said mildly. "My team is focused on making this as seamless as possible. I'll continue to coordinate with your security forces to ensure the safety of the relics."

Michael nodded, glancing at Ferrante, who seemed increasingly comfortable with Voss's presence. It was true—since Voss had become involved, there had been fewer headaches and logistical obstacles. Everything was running according to plan, with a kind of efficiency the Vatican rarely experienced in such large-scale events.

"Good," Michael said, still keeping his tone measured. "Security is, of course, our top priority. We can't afford any lapses."

"Absolutely," Voss agreed smoothly. "I understand the sensitivity of this exhibition. Rest assured, my focus remains on making sure everything runs flawlessly, both in terms of exposure and in terms of safeguarding the sanctity of the relics."

Michael couldn't help but feel a slight unease, even in the face of Voss's apparent competence. The man's words were always perfect, his demeanor always calm, but there was a layer beneath it—a quiet confidence that spoke of deeper machinations. Still, it was hard to argue with success, and in this moment, it seemed as if Voss had delivered precisely what he promised: maximum exposure, global interest, and streamlined efficiency.

Ferrante, clearly satisfied, leaned back with a rare

smile. "You've done well, Mr. Voss. If this continues, I'm sure the exhibition will be a remarkable success."

Voss inclined his head, his expression one of modest humility. "I'm honored to be a part of it, Monsignor. The relics deserve nothing less."

Michael nodded, his eyes narrowing slightly as he watched Voss collect his papers, all while maintaining that air of unruffled professionalism. For now, it seemed, Voss was content to stay in his lane, providing just enough expertise to keep everyone satisfied. But Michael had been around long enough to know that even the smallest hint of control, once ceded, could become something far more dangerous.

As the meeting concluded and they rose to leave, Ferrante reached out to shake Voss's hand. Michael followed suit, feeling the cool, steady grip of Voss's fingers. They exchanged pleasantries, the air in the room lighter now that the formalities were over. Yet as Voss turned to leave, Michael couldn't shake the feeling that they were only seeing a fraction of what the man intended.

CHAPTER

TWENTY

T he morning light filtered gently through the tall windows of the Pio Reading Room, casting a soft glow over the shelves of ancient volumes and manuscripts. Simon Ginzberg sat at the table, his fingers nervously tapping against the wood as he stared at nothing in particular. His thoughts were on Emilio Rossi—his colleague, his friend. Gone. Killed in a car accident just when he had been on the verge of revealing something important. Simon's heart tightened at the thought of it, and with each passing moment, the feeling that Emilio's death wasn't an accident gnawed at him.

The door to the reading room opened quietly, and Father Michael Dominic stepped in, his expression calm but alert. He approached Simon with the same air of controlled precision that had made him the perfect man to guard the Vatican's secrets. Michael sat down across from Simon, sensing the weight of the situation before a word had even been spoken.

"Simon," Michael began, his voice steady. "I came as soon as I could. You said this was important."

Simon exhaled slowly, trying to collect himself, his mind still reeling. "Yes, thank you for coming, Michael. I... This wasn't supposed to happen like this. The man I was supposed to meet with two days ago, Dr. Emilio Rossi—he's dead. A car accident, they say. But..." He faltered, shaking his head. "I'm not sure I believe that anymore."

Michael's eyes sharpened at the mention of Rossi. "I'm sorry to hear about Dr. Rossi. I know of his work. A loss like that, especially right now... It must feel impossible." He paused, studying Simon's expression. "But you don't think it was an accident?"

Simon shook his head, grief and frustration mixed in his voice. "No, I don't. Emilio was meticulous, careful. He'd been working on something—something big, something that made him nervous. He wouldn't have been careless. And now... he's dead. When his daughter called to give me the news, she told me that the police are considering foul play. I didn't connect that with his interest in seeing me at that moment, but since then it has coalesced in my mind."

Michael leaned forward, his brow furrowing. "What was he working on?"

Simon took a deep breath, his eyes clouded with uncertainty. "That's the thing. He didn't get the chance to tell me everything. But it had to do with bones. He told me that much before... before the accident. He was worried about replication—about someone making copies of relics; bones specifically. He was concerned that something dangerous was happening, and he mentioned Dr. Helena Barrett."

At the sound of Helena's name, Michael's jaw tightened. His unease with her had always been subtle, but real. She was known for her skill in artifact replication, but her involvement in something dangerous? "Helena Barrett..." he murmured. "But why would she be involved in replicating bones?"

Simon leaned forward, lowering his voice. "I don't know, but Emilio was certain she was connected to it somehow. He said she was working with someone powerful—someone who wanted to keep things hidden. He didn't name anyone else, but it was enough to scare him. He told me that they were replicating bones for some reason, but he didn't get the chance to explain why."

Michael's thoughts churned, trying to piece together the fragments of the puzzle. Replication—it made sense in Helena's line of work. But replicating relics, and specifically bones? For what purpose? A chill ran down his spine as his mind suddenly flicked to the forthcoming exhibition, the monumental event centered around the public display of St. Peter's bones. Could this be connected?

"You said Emilio was talking about bones," he said slowly, the words hanging in the air. "With the exhibition of St. Peter's relics coming up... are you saying he thought someone might be replicating *those* bones?"

Simon hesitated, his eyes meeting Michael's. "He never said St. Peter's name directly," he clarified, "but with the timing of everything—the bones being prepared for display and the secrecy around it—it's hard not to connect the dots. He did say '*And not just any bones.*' What if... what if someone was replicating the bones to switch them? To make it seem like the bones being displayed are authentic, while the real ones are taken?"

The air in the room seemed to grow colder as the implications of Simon's words settled in. Michael's pulse quickened, his mind racing. St. Peter's bones. If someone had managed to replicate them, to replace them with fakes... the consequences would be catastrophic. Not only would it undermine the credibility of the exhibition, but it would call into question the integrity of the Vatican itself.

And worse, if someone powerful enough to pull this off was behind it, then Emilio's death was no accident.

Michael stood abruptly, walking over to the window, staring out as if the answer might materialize in the city of Rome sprawling beyond. "Replicating St. Peter's bones..." he whispered, the thought almost too terrible to voice. "If that's what's happening—if someone is planning to switch them before the exhibition..."

He turned back to Simon, his eyes dark with the gravity of the situation. "That would be unthinkable. A deception of this scale... it's inconceivable."

Simon's voice trembled slightly as he spoke. "That's why I'm so worried, Michael. If Emilio was right, and if he was killed to protect this secret, then whoever's behind it won't stop. They're willing to do whatever it takes to keep this covered up."

Michael was silent for a long moment, his thoughts spinning as he tried to grasp the enormity of what Simon was saying. If St. Peter's bones were the target, if they were being switched with replicas, then this wasn't just a matter of relics—it was a direct attack on the Church's authority, its history, its very identity.

He exhaled slowly, his resolve hardening. "I need to speak with Barrett," he said finally. "But I can't let her know what we're suspecting. If she's involved, I'll need to approach this carefully, without tipping her off."

Simon nodded. "Emilio's death... it could mean he got too close. I think we should be careful here. I don't know how far this goes."

Michael gave a brief nod, his mind already turning over the best way to approach Helena. He needed to find out what she knew—what her role in this was—without letting her realize he was onto her. If there was indeed a plan to switch the bones, he needed to stop it before the exhibition. But he also needed to tread carefully. If someone were willing to kill to protect this secret, then they wouldn't hesitate to strike again.

"I'll be careful," Michael said, his voice low. "But I can't let this go. If St. Peter's bones are at risk, if someone's tampering with them, then I need to find out the truth. Whatever the cost."

As Michael turned to leave, the weight of the situation bore down on him. Emilio's death, the looming exhibition, and the potential conspiracy threatening the

Vatican—it all felt overwhelming. But he knew he had no choice.

As he walked out of the Pio Reading Room, a chill ran down his spine. He couldn't shake the feeling that time was running out—and that whoever was behind this was already one step ahead.

TWENTY-ONE

Michael walked down a quiet street in the heart of Rome, away from the bustle of Vatican City. He had arranged a meeting with Dr. Helena Barrett, whom he knew only by reputation under the pretext of academic curiosity. Her home office, a modest but sophisticated space tucked into an old building in the historic center, wasn't far from the Vatican, but it felt worlds apart from the sanctity of the Holy See. Michael knew this meeting was delicate—he had to be careful not to reveal too much of his own suspicions while probing her activities.

As he approached the unassuming building, he felt a tension tightening in his chest. Emilio Rossi's sudden death and his vague warning about Barrett weighed heavily on his mind. What had Emilio found, and how much had he managed to uncover before his tragic accident? Helena Barrett had been mentioned, and now it was Michael's turn to find out why.

He rang the bell, and after a brief pause, a soft click echoed from the door, signaling it was unlocked. He pushed it open and stepped inside, greeted by the cool air and the scent of old books and polished wood. Helena's loft was on the second floor, a space that, according to her reputation, served both as a workspace and a hub of intricate academic projects.

Dr. Barrett greeted him at her door, her face composed, her eyes sharp and observant behind her glasses. She was a woman of quiet elegance— meticulous in her appearance and, as Michael expected, in her work. The office reflected her precision. The room was lined with books on archaeology, historical texts, and tools of her trade—small instruments, 3D models, and even a few carefully arranged relics or replicas on display.

"Father Dominic," Helena said with a polite smile, stepping aside to welcome him in. "I'm glad to meet you finally. Please, have a seat."

"Thank you, Dr. Barrett," Michael replied as he entered. He took in the carefully curated environment as he sat, noticing the neat stacks of papers and the delicate tools on the desk—evidence of a master in her field. This was a woman accustomed to control, someone who understood the balance between art and science.

"I've been eager to meet with you," he began, maintaining a friendly tone. "Your work has fascinated me for some time. Artifact replication, especially when it comes to sensitive relics, is an area I find both academically and spiritually significant."

Helena smiled slightly, her posture remaining

poised. "I'm glad to hear that. It's a field that requires not only precision but a deep respect for the past. I take great care with each piece I work on."

Michael nodded, leaning in slightly. "It must be a delicate balance—capturing the authenticity of the original without crossing any ethical lines, especially with something as important as religious relics."

Her eyes flickered for the briefest of moments, but she maintained her calm. "That's true. Replication is a tool for preservation and study, but I'm always aware of the weight of what I'm working with. In cases where relics are involved, authenticity must remain paramount."

Michael kept his tone casual, his posture relaxed. "I imagine the bones of St. Peter must have crossed your mind, given the upcoming exhibition. Have you ever been consulted on something so significant?"

Helena's smile remained polite, though her response was more measured. "I've heard much about the exhibition, of course, but I haven't been involved directly. I imagine the Vatican has its own internal processes for handling such relics. If the Vatican ever required my services for something as sacred as St. Peter's bones, I would be honored, of course..." She smiled as if finding a clear path to avoid road bumps in his questioning. "Do I dare ask if you are requesting such services from me?"

Michael smiled as well, aware she'd played their dialogue game skillfully. "No, I'm afraid not. However, you would certainly be highly considered if that were to become the case. The Vatican always looks to improve how we handle and preserve our artifacts. Considering our upcoming event for St. Peter's bones, I hoped to mine some of your expertise for a few moments. People's faith is tied so closely to these artifacts that we want the best process for preservation. Already, we have taken unprecedented heightened security measures, which I'm sure you can appreciate."

Two can play at this dialogue game, he thought.

Helena's smile wasn't reflected in her eyes, but her voice remained steady. "Of course. The Church has always taken relics seriously. It's why replication is such a valuable tool—to preserve the originals while allowing study and admiration of their likeness." She then proceeded to explain her methods of preservation and care of genuine relics and the usefulness, at times, of replicas to be used for academic and religious displays.

Afterward, they sat in silence for a moment, the conversation hanging between them like a thread waiting to be tugged. Michael sensed he had pushed as far as he could without tipping his hand. Helena was careful, but her guardedness around the topic of the bones was telling. She wasn't likely to admit anything, but the subtleties of her responses gave Michael enough to continue his investigation.

"I appreciate your time, Dr. Barrett," Michael said finally, easing back into a more casual tone. "Your insights into replication are invaluable. I've learned a great deal from our conversation."

Helena relaxed slightly, though her smile remained polite and distant. "I'm always happy to discuss my work, Father Dominic. It's not every day I get to speak with someone who understands the spiritual weight behind what we do."

Michael stood, extending his hand. "Incidentally, you were a colleague of Dr. Emilio Rossi, weren't you?"

Helena froze at the mention of Emilio's name, her expression shifting from surprise to confusion. But it wasn't just the name that startled her—it was the way Michael had referred to him in the past tense, a subtle yet telling choice of words that sent a chill down her spine.

"Yes, Emilio and I are colleagues," she said, her voice hesitant, as if trying to mask the sudden unease creeping into her tone. Her brows knitted. "But... has something happened to him?"

Michael's expression softened, his voice carefully measured. "I suppose you hadn't heard," he said gently, watching her reaction closely. "Emilio was killed in a car accident a couple of days ago."

For a moment, Helena said nothing, her face blank as if the words hadn't fully registered. Then, like a wave crashing over her, the meaning sank in. Her face turned ashen, all color draining away. She swayed slightly, her hand instinctively gripping the edge of the table for support.

"No," she breathed, the word barely audible. Her knees felt unsteady, and she stumbled forward, her free hand reaching out to Michael as if he were the only solid thing in a world suddenly spinning off its axis.

Michael caught her by the elbow, steadying her. "Helena," he said, his tone low and reassuring, "are you all right?"

She clutched his hand tightly, her fingers trembling against his. "No, I hadn't heard," she managed, her voice breaking. Her usually composed demeanor was gone, replaced by raw, unguarded emotion. "How awful... Emilio..."

Michael led her gently to a chair, urging her to sit. "Take a moment," he said, his voice soft but insistent. "I know this is a shock."

Helena sank into the seat, her hand still clutching Michael's. Her mind reeled, fragments of memory and unspoken thoughts about Emilio tumbling chaotically. Though their relationship had been purely professional, there was something about his sudden, tragic absence that hit her deeply, stirring emotions she hadn't anticipated.

"I can't believe it," she said, her voice barely above a whisper. "He was so... alive. We were just working on something together. I can't wrap my head around it."

Michael nodded solemnly, his gaze steady on her. "I understand. It's never easy to process something like this."

Helena took a shuddering breath, willing herself to regain composure. As she leaned back in the chair, a flicker of realization crossed her face, something almost imperceptible but not lost on Michael.

Her grip on his hand loosened slightly as she glanced up, her eyes shadowed with something beyond grief—something closer to fear. "Do they know... what caused the accident?" she asked hesitantly, her voice laced with unease.

Michael hesitated, choosing his words carefully. "It's

being investigated, but so far, they believe foul play may have been involved."

Helena nodded slowly, though her gaze drifted as if she were lost in thought, calculating, perhaps, or remembering something she didn't want to share.

Michael watched her closely, filing away the subtle shifts in her demeanor. Her reaction to Emilio's death was more than grief—it carried the weight of someone who knew there was more to the story than she could admit.

"Helena," he said gently, leaning forward, "if there's anything you know, anything you think could be important..."

She straightened, her composure slipping back into place like a mask. "No," she said quickly, shaking her head. "No, I—I can't imagine what there would be. He never mentioned anything unusual."

Michael nodded slowly, but his suspicion deepened. There was something Helena wasn't saying, and he intended to find out what.

"Perhaps we'll have more to discuss in the future," Michael said, lightening the tone. "The Vatican always looks to improve how we handle and preserve our artifacts."

Helena shook his hand, her grip now firm. "I look forward to it."

As Michael left her office and stepped back onto the busy streets of Rome, the weight of the conversation lingered in his mind. Helena had been careful, but there was something in how she responded—just enough to suggest she wasn't telling him everything. Whatever

Emilio had uncovered, it involved her, and now Michael was certain that the path to the truth would lead him deeper into her carefully guarded world.

But he also knew that Helena wasn't likely to make a mistake easily. She was too skilled, too precise. If Michael wanted to find out the full truth, he would need to play the long game, watching for any slip, any misstep that could reveal what she was hiding.

As he walked back toward the Vatican, he knew this was only the beginning of a much larger, more dangerous investigation.

As the door to her office clicked shut behind Father Michael, Helena Barrett stood still for a moment, her pulse quickening. She moved to her desk with deliberate slowness, her hands resting on the edge as she stared at the papers and tools scattered across its surface. The conversation had been polite, measured, but there was no mistaking the underlying tension in Father Dominic's questions. He hadn't come just for academic curiosity—he was probing, feeling for something beneath the surface.

Helena's mind raced as she replayed the encounter. His mention of the bones—the pointed mention of St. Peter's bones—was too specific to be casual. She had been careful, keeping her answers controlled and professional, but had she said too much? And her reaction to word of Emilio's death, Michael had to have seen that… She rubbed her fingers together as if trying to wipe away the anxiety crawling under her skin.

She moved quickly to her window, looking out over the narrow street below. The city continued as if nothing had changed, but Helena knew better. Father Michael was getting too close—closer than anyone should. And if he suspected anything about what was happening with the bones or Emilio's death, she wasn't sure how much longer she could maintain her composure. She had to act, and fast.

CHAPTER
TWENTY-TWO

Helena Barrett's hands trembled as she dialed Elliot Voss's private number, her nerves fraying with each passing second. The conversation with Father Michael Dominic earlier had been far too probing, and her calm façade had barely held. She could feel it—Michael wasn't just asking idle questions. He knew something, or at least suspected it. The moment Voss answered, his voice smooth and composed as always, she could barely keep the tension from her voice.

"Elliot, we need to talk," she said, her words spilling out in a rush. "Michael Dominic came to see me today. He was asking questions—too many questions about the bones. He was subtle, but I could tell he's onto something."

There was a brief silence on the other end before Voss spoke, his tone low and measured. "Tell me everything. What exactly did he ask?"

Helena quickly recounted the conversation, her anxiety rising as she went through each pointed question Michael had asked about her replication work and how he had steered the conversation toward the bones of St. Peter. When she finished, there was another pause. This one felt heavier, more dangerous.

"Michael Dominic…" Voss's voice was calmer than she expected. "He's sharp, I'll give him that. But he hasn't outright accused you of anything, has he?"

"No, not directly," Helena replied, pacing her office. "But it's only a matter of time. He knows I'm involved—he suspects. And I'm not going to let myself be the one who falls if this whole thing comes crashing down."

Voss's voice hardened. "Calm down, Helena. You're in too deep to pull out now. If you even try, it'll only raise more suspicions. We can't afford to have Dominic digging deeper into this. We need to control the narrative before he does."

Helena stopped pacing, her pulse racing. "What are you suggesting? He's already circling—if he presses further, I don't know how much longer I can hold him off."

Voss's mind was already working through a solution, his fingers drumming softly against his desk. "We need to distract him. He's suspicious, but his focus is still too broad. What if we give him something to chase, something that keeps him busy and steers him away from the bones?"

Helena frowned, uncertain. "And how do we do that without making it obvious?"

Voss leaned back in his chair, a faint smile playing at

his lips as an idea took shape. "We give him a different relic to question. Something minor enough to be plausible, but significant enough to hold his attention for a while. We create the appearance of another potential project—something far enough from the bones to keep his focus elsewhere. We let him believe he's onto something, while we ensure that the real secret stays buried."

Helena hesitated, the plan sinking in. "But where do we find something like that?"

"I'll handle that part," Voss said smoothly. "There are plenty of artifacts floating around the Vatican Archives, and not all of them have the same scrutiny as St. Peter's. We create just enough doubt to make it look like someone's playing a game with relics, and Dominic will go sniffing in the wrong direction."

Helena bit her lip, still jittery. "What if he doesn't take the bait? What if he keeps coming after me?"

Voss's voice was ice now, his control slipping just enough for her to hear the edge in it. "He will, Helena. I know his type. You just need to stay calm and stick to your story. If you panic now, you'll give him exactly what he needs."

She swallowed hard, the weight of his words settling over her. She didn't have much of a choice—Voss was right. She was in too deep. Pulling out now would only make her a target. "Fine. But you'd better make sure this works."

"It will," Voss said confidently. "Just be patient. I'll take care of everything."

As Helena ended the call, her heart still pounded in

her chest, but she felt a sliver of reassurance. Voss had a plan, and if anyone could divert Father Michael's suspicions, it was him. All she had to do now was stay calm and hope that the smoke screen they were about to create would be enough to keep the priest off their trail.

For now, at least.

CHAPTER
TWENTY-THREE

F ather Michael Dominic sat at his desk in his apartment in Domus Santa Marta, the quiet of the late evening a rare reprieve from the storm of thoughts swirling through his mind. The warm, golden glow of the desk lamp threw shadows across the worn pages of ancient texts scattered before him, but he barely saw them. His mind, usually sharp and focused, was now frayed at the edges, weighed down by too many competing concerns.

The Peter-Linus inscription gnawed at him like a splinter in his thoughts. It was as if the ancient stone itself was pressing on him, daring him to unravel its mystery. He knew that what Marcus Russo was uncovering could be more than just a historical curiosity. Matteo had kept him updated ever since, as he and his crew had worked overtime to uncover anything else that fit with these texts. If substantiated with more scripts, this had the potential to disrupt centuries of belief, to challenge the very foundations of the Church's authority. And then there was the more immediate and pressing matter: the bones of St. Peter—the sacred relics that had been entrusted to him. Could it be true that someone was preparing to switch them with replicas? How could such a sacrilege be allowed to take root right under his nose?

And, of course, there was Elliot Voss.

Michael leaned back in his chair, running a hand through his hair. Voss's involvement in the exhibition had to be a condition of his offer to assist with all future Vatican Archives digitization, and the financial boost to the Secret Archives as well. Michael had taken his interest in the upcoming event as just Voss's way to show off his abilities with the media at the outset of their cooperative venture. Or was there more to it? Was Voss weaving himself deeper into the Vatican's affairs, using the forthcoming exhibition as a stage for something that Michael couldn't quite put his finger on yet?

He sighed deeply, the tension in his shoulders aching as he stared blankly at the dim outlines of the buildings outside his window. Rome at night, the Eternal City, a place of both solace and burden. His thoughts drifted, unbidden, to Hana.

He hadn't seen her in days, though her presence was always with him, just beneath the surface of his thoughts. The last time they had met, over wine at Paisano Trattoria, there had been a warmth between them—a growing intimacy that neither of them had dared to fully acknowledge. Michael felt it now, a quiet tug on his heart, a pull that both comforted and unsettled him. She was a journalist, sharp, courageous, unafraid of the truth no matter where it led her. And he —he was a priest. He had been ordained with the clear understanding that his life would be one of service, of devotion to God and the Church, unencumbered by the complexities of personal relationships.

But that had been before Pope Ignatius's dictum, the one that had altered the fabric of the Church in ways still rippling through the clergy. Priests were now allowed to marry. Theologically, it made sense to Michael. Marriage was a sacrament, a path to holiness in its own right, a reflection of God's love for humanity. But for himself? The decision seemed impossible to grasp.

Michael closed his eyes and leaned forward, resting his forehead in his hands. Could he even imagine such a life for himself? Could he, a man who had spent his entire adult life in the Church, really balance the weight of his spiritual duties with the demands of a relationship—of marriage? He had spent so many years alone, focused on his vocation, on uncovering the past to serve the present. The idea of sharing his life, his fears, his joys, with another person felt both foreign and terrifying.

And yet, when he thought of Hana, something within him stirred. There was a tenderness in her and a strength he admired. She saw him not as a priest, not as some distant figure of authority, but as a man—Michael: flawed and questioning, vulnerable in ways he hadn't been with anyone in a long time. But did she understand the weight of what she was stepping into? Could she?

He stood and walked to the window, pressing his palm against the cool glass, watching the faint movement of the city below. The Church had always asked much of its servants, and he had accepted that. But now, it asked something else—something more complicated. Pope Ignatius's pronouncement had opened a door that had been shut for centuries, but just because the door was open, it didn't mean he was ready to walk through it. And even if he were, what would Hana say? Was she ready for the life he led, a life full of secrets, ancient mysteries, and relentless obligations?

Michael knew the question wasn't simply about whether he could love her—he knew he did, though the admission sat heavy in his chest. The real question was whether he could love her *and* serve the Church. Could he do both without sacrificing the heart of either? His life had always been one of compartmentalization—work, faith, duty, all neatly aligned. But Hana had blurred those lines in ways he hadn't anticipated. She had made him question whether there was more to life than the rigid structure he had always adhered to.

He thought again of the inscription, of Peter and Linus, of power and authority, of the fragility of truth. He was standing at a crossroads, not only in his professional life but in his personal one. The weight of both decisions pressed in on him, leaving him no room to breathe.

The Church had changed, but had he? Could he change?

Michael stepped back from the window and returned to his desk. His eyes fell on a small, framed photograph—a candid shot of him and Hana, taken at a book launch a year ago. They were smiling, her arm casually resting on his shoulder, and for a moment, the world had seemed simple. They had been friends then, colleagues even, before this... tension had crept into the spaces between them.

He sighed. Whether he was ready for it or not, the decision would come. He only hoped, when the time came, he would have the clarity to make the right one. For both of them.

But for now, all he could do was wait—and pray. Pray for guidance, for peace, for the strength to face whatever lay ahead.

CHAPTER
TWENTY-FOUR

The next morning, Michael sat at his desk in the Apostolic Archives, staring down at the piles of documents and reports, but his mind wasn't on them. His thoughts were caught in the web of suspicion and confusion that had been building since Emilio Rossi's cryptic warning. Rossi had been certain that something was wrong with St. Peter's bones, that there was a deception surrounding them. And now, with Rossi dead, Michael couldn't shake the feeling that time was running out.

The Vatican's relics were authentic. Michael knew that. There was no question about the bones that had been resting in St. Peter's tomb for centuries. His concern wasn't about the authenticity of the relics, but about a plot—a hidden agenda to possibly switch them. And every thread he pulled seemed to lead back to Elliot Voss and Helena Barrett.

Michael didn't trust Helena. Her work in artifact

replication had always made him uneasy, her proximity to bones in particular a little too convenient. She was skilled, no doubt, but there was something about her— an aura of secrecy that made him wary. But until now, he hadn't been able to pinpoint exactly why. And that uncertainty gnawed at him.

His phone rang, jolting him from his thoughts. The caller ID showed Helena's name, and a knot formed in his stomach. He hesitated before answering, the coincidence of her timing and his distrust flickering in the back of his mind.

"Father Dominic?" Helena's voice came through the line, calm but with an undercurrent of something— anxiety, perhaps? "I need to talk to you. There's something I should've told you earlier."

Michael's jaw clenched as he leaned back in his chair, feeling the familiar tension rise in his chest. "Go on," he said, his tone measured, masking the distrust simmering beneath.

Helena's voice wavered slightly as if choosing her words carefully. "It's about the bones I've been working on. They're not what you might think."

Michael felt a sharp chill creep up his spine. *What had she done?*

"I haven't been working on St. Peter's bones, as I think you might have suspected," Helena continued. "The bones I've been handling—they belong to someone else. Another Peter."

Michael's eyes narrowed, his distrust sharpening into something colder. "Another Peter?" he repeated, his voice hard.

Helena hesitated, her breath audible on the other end of the line. "Yes. I was hired privately to handle a set of bones—belonging to an early Christian martyr named Peter the Exorcist. He's not widely known, but he was important to some smaller circles of collectors. I've been cleaning and processing them for a private display. These bones have nothing to do with the Vatican or St. Peter's relics. I wasn't replicating anything. I wasn't involved in any issues you might have been worried about. But it has bothered me that I didn't simply tell you what I'm working on."

Michael's mind raced, the puzzle pieces slowly falling into place. Helena's work had been private, unconnected to the Vatican's relics, as Peter the Exorcist's bones were not among the artifacts held by the Vatican. But why had this come up now? Why had Emilio Rossi been so adamant that something was wrong with the bones?

"You're telling me that while the Vatican is preparing to display St. Peter's bones, you've been handling another set of relics for a private client? And you didn't think to mention this earlier?" Michael's voice was tight, his distrust spilling over.

Helena's voice softened, almost pleading. "I should have, of course, but I didn't want to confuse things. And I do try to be discreet about my private clientele's commissions. But later, I realized I should've said something…"

Michael closed his eyes, feeling the weight of her words sink in. She was being careful—too careful.

Could she be telling the truth? Or was this just another layer of deception?

"I was flattered at first to think the Vatican might need my expertise in replicating St. Peter's bones, but the coincidence of that potential offer and my current work on Peter the Exorcist's bones, well..." Helena said quietly, her voice almost trembling. "I began to think you thought I was working on replicating St. Peter's bones. I just felt too uncomfortable to say anything at the time. I hope you understand. But I also hope to leave the door open to work with the Vatican someday, so I wanted to clarify to you that the bones I'm working on aren't part of the Vatican's relics but from a lesser-known martyr, someone important to a small group of collectors, as I said."

A coincidence. Michael didn't believe in coincidences, not in the Vatican. Not when it came to relics, and certainly not when it involved people like Voss and Helena Barrett. But he knew that pressing her further wouldn't get him any closer to the truth. She was either telling the truth, or she was very good at covering her tracks.

"Why are you telling me this now?" Michael asked, his voice sharp. "If these bones have nothing to do with the Vatican or St. Peter's relics, why come forward now?"

Helena was silent for a long moment, as though weighing her next words carefully. "Because, Michael... I had to wonder why you even considered I was involved in St. Peter's bones. I ended up suspecting someone's been manipulating you. I don't know who, or why, but possibly it is to make you think there's something going on when really something else may be going on."

Michael's heart pounded in his chest. Had he been chasing a lie? Had someone misled Emilio from the outset? Had they wanted Emilio—and whoever he contacted—to doubt the bones, to get lost in the mystery of an unrelated relic as a distraction?

And now, with Helena's confession, Michael knew he had to shift his focus. The real plot, the real conspiracy, lay not in the relics themselves, but in the distraction they had created. Someone planted the seeds of distrust in Emilio in order to distract anyone then involved in the event from looking too closely at other aspects of the exhibition.

He gripped the phone tightly, his voice cold. "Helena, if you're lying to me—if this is a game— believe me, I will find out. And when I do, it won't end well for you."

"I'm not lying, Michael," Helena said, her voice steady despite the tension in the air. "I have nothing to do with the Vatican relics. Whoever's behind making you suspicious of me wants you to look in the wrong place. Be careful."

Michael hung up the phone without another word, his mind already turning to the next steps. They all had been led down a false trail, and it was time to get back on track. The facts were clear: someone had made Emilio concerned and when he tried to figure it out, they had killed him. So the real and deadly deception was still out there, lurking in the shadows of the Vatican.

And now, more than ever, he was determined to find it.

With renewed purpose, Michael stood and gathered his things. He needed to follow the leads that Emilio had left behind, but now, with the clarity that came from Helena's admission, he had a new sense of where to start.

TWENTY-FIVE

The air in the catacombs beneath St. Peter's Basilica was cool and damp, the scent of ancient stone and earth filling the narrow passageways. The low hum of distant voices and movement from the Vatican above seemed a world away from this underground labyrinth of history and mystery. Marcus Russo crouched low, his gloved hands sifting through the dirt and rubble of an ancient burial site, his breath steady as he worked. Beside him, Sofia knelt, her brow furrowed in concentration as she meticulously cleared the earth from the edges of what appeared to be a grave marker.

"Here," Marcus whispered, motioning toward a particularly rough patch of stone just beneath the surface. "This could be it."

They had been searching for hours, combing through the catacombs for any sign of the elusive grave of Linus, the second pope and Peter's successor. But it wasn't just

Linus's burial they sought—it was the truth about the mysterious and little-understood relationship between Linus and Peter that had drawn them here. And perhaps, something deeper.

Sofia paused, brushing a loose strand of hair from her face and glancing at Marcus. "You really think we'll find it?"

Marcus didn't answer immediately, his eyes locked on the stone he was now clearing. It was larger than the others they had uncovered, its edges worn smooth by centuries of earth and time. The symbols etched into its surface were faint, almost erased by the ages. But they were there. He could feel it.

"I don't know," he finally said, his voice low and filled with the weight of uncertainty. "But we've come this far. If there's any place we'll find answers, it's here."

They worked in silence for several minutes more, their movements careful, deliberate. Small stones and dust crumbled away as they uncovered more of the grave marker. As the last layer of dirt fell away, Marcus let out a quiet breath. There it was, another inscription, much like the one they had discovered days ago. The script was unfamiliar at first glance, but as Marcus studied it, his pulse quickened.

"This is Brythonic," he said, his voice barely more than a murmur. He wiped the rest of the grime from the stone, revealing a line of carved text that sent a jolt of excitement through him.

Sofia leaned closer, squinting at the inscription. "Brythonic... like the other one."

Marcus nodded, already reaching for his notebook.

The first inscription they had found had been a revelation, an ancient script that hinted at a deeper connection between Linus and Peter. But this one—this one seemed to promise even more.

As Marcus traced the letters with his finger, he began transcribing them into his notebook. The symbols were simple, yet their meaning felt profound, though he couldn't yet understand them fully. He would need Michael to help with the translation, but already, the words tugged at something in his memory. It felt like they were on the brink of uncovering something extraordinary.

"What does it say?" Sofia asked, her voice hushed.

"I can't translate it all," Marcus admitted, his fingers moving quickly across the page as he copied the inscription. "But it's about Linus. It mentions his role alongside Peter."

Sofia's eyes widened. "You mean… confirming that Linus was more than just Peter's successor?"

Marcus nodded. "Yes. This could be the key to understanding the nature of their leadership. Maybe even to resolving the mystery of whether Linus was meant to be Peter's equal, his alternate in leading the early Church."

His hands trembled slightly as he finished copying the last symbol. The inscription, now clearly visible on the stone, seemed to shimmer in the faint light of their lanterns, as though the truth buried for centuries was finally ready to come to light.

He read the Brythonic text aloud, though the words felt foreign on his tongue:

GARY MCAVOY

"'*Linus ocus Petros na ledagh an sluagh na solas. Brathair di an carraig, ed ar ar bonnci keifur. Cynt afron nhw yn cadw'r praidd.*'"

"'Linus, with Peter…' something something… 'leads the chosen to…' something. 'Brother to the rock, he is the foundation's keeper…' I can't make out the rest," Marcus finished. "That's a job for Father Dominic."

He sat back on his heels, his heart racing. "This… this confirms it. Linus wasn't just a follower of Peter— he was meant to lead with him somehow."

Sofia stared at the inscription, her face a mixture of awe and disbelief. "We need to take this to Father Dominic. He'll be able to help us figure out the full translation."

Marcus stood, the notebook clutched tightly in his hand. "Michael needs to see this right away. This changes everything we know about the early Church."

He took a final look at the grave marker before gathering his tools. The inscription they had uncovered would need to be carefully analyzed, and the significance of what it revealed was staggering. Linus, the supposed second pope, had been a co-leader with Peter, a hidden figure in the Church's earliest days whose role had been obscured by time.

As they prepared to leave the catacombs, Marcus couldn't shake the feeling that this was just the beginning. The inscription, with its ancient Brythonic script, seemed to hint at something far more complex than they had anticipated. And now, with this new discovery, they were one step closer to uncovering the truth.

They moved quickly through the narrow corridors of the catacombs, their path lit only by the dim glow of their lanterns. Above them, the Vatican continued its preparations for the grand exhibition. But down here, in the quiet and forgotten tombs, another story was emerging—one that had been buried for centuries.

CHAPTER

TWENTY-SIX

T he sun hung low in the sky as Marcus made his way through the narrow, twisting corridors of the Vatican, the worn leather notebook clutched tightly in his hands. His mind raced, replaying the discovery from the catacombs over and over. The inscription—the cryptic Brythonic text etched into the ancient stone—seemed to reverberate with meaning far beyond what he could decipher. He needed answers, and he knew exactly where to go.

Father Michael Dominic's office, tucked away deep within the Vatican's labyrinthine halls, had become something of a sanctuary for Marcus in recent months. The Prefect of the Secret Archives was one of the few people Marcus trusted implicitly, especially with matters as delicate as this. As he approached the door, he hesitated for a moment, collecting his thoughts before raising a hand to knock.

"Come in," came Michael's voice, calm but commanding, from within.

Marcus pushed open the heavy wooden door and stepped inside. The room was dimly lit, a golden shaft of evening light streaming through the high window behind Michael's desk. The priest sat there, his head bent over a stack of budget reports, absorbed in his work. He glanced up as Marcus entered, his expression shifting from curiosity to concern at the sight of the archaeologist's tense demeanor.

"Marcus," Michael said, sitting up straighter, sensing the urgency. "What have you found?"

Without a word, Marcus crossed the room and laid the notebook on the desk, flipping it open to the page where he had copied the inscription. The worn Brythonic letters stared up from the page, each one carefully transcribed from the grave marker they had uncovered. Marcus gestured toward the text, his voice low but charged with emotion.

"We found it. Another inscription. It was buried deep in the catacombs, near what we believe could be Linus's grave." He paused, looking Michael squarely in the eyes. "This one is even more explicit. It mentions Peter—and Linus—leading the early Church together."

Michael's expression darkened as he leaned forward, scanning the inscription. His fingers hovered over the text, his eyes narrowing as he mouthed the ancient words. The Brythonic script was archaic, but Michael had seen variations of it before. Still, it took him several moments to fully grasp the meaning. When he did, his face paled slightly, his brows knitting together in a mix of disbelief and deep concern.

"Read it aloud. Please," Marcus urged, his voice tight with anticipation.

Michael hesitated, the weight of the inscription clearly bearing down on him, before he began to speak, his voice soft but steady.

"It says, 'Linus, with Peter at his side, leads the chosen to the light. Brother to the rock, he is the foundation's keeper. Together, they bind the flock.'"

He stopped, his hand resting on the edge of the desk as if he needed to brace himself. The silence that followed was thick, almost suffocating. Marcus could feel his heart pounding in his chest, the tension between them growing by the second. He felt a shiver run down his spine.

Hearing the translation aloud was different—it felt more real, more dangerous. The implications were staggering. If this inscription was accurate, it suggested something far more profound than a simple succession of leadership. It implied a partnership, a shared authority between Peter and Linus in the Church's formative years. Linus hadn't merely followed Peter— he had stood beside him. In fact, it could appear as if Linus was the leader between the two in the first line.

Michael leaned back in his chair, his hands clasped tightly together in front of him, his expression tense. For a moment, neither of them spoke, the weight of the discovery settling heavily over the room.

"This changes everything, doesn't it?" Marcus finally asked, his voice barely above a whisper.

Michael's gaze remained fixed on the notebook, as if the answer could be found hidden between the lines of the ancient text. "If this inscription is genuine—and it appears to be—it raises more questions than it answers," he said, his voice edged with unease. "This suggests that Linus's role in the early Church wasn't merely that of a successor, but of a co-leader… perhaps even a foundational figure with Peter 'at his side,' potentially meaning secondary. The phrase 'brother to the rock'—it's unmistakable. It connects Linus to Peter's very identity as the rock upon which the Church was built."

Marcus nodded, his excitement tempered by the gravity of Michael's words. "Exactly. And the part about 'binding the flock'—that's not language used casually. It implies authority. Real authority. They led together."

Michael slowly closed the notebook, his fingers tracing the edge of the cover as he processed the information. "But why has this remained hidden? Why wasn't this aspect of Linus's role preserved in the official history of the Church? We know so little about Linus, but to discover this now…" He trailed off, his thoughts racing.

Marcus shifted in his seat, leaning forward. "Do you think it was deliberately suppressed? Or simply forgotten over the centuries? Either way, it changes how we understand the early Church. It wasn't just Peter laying the foundations. Linus was there too."

Michael let out a slow breath, the weight of the discovery pressing on him more heavily now. "I don't know. There could have been theological or political reasons to emphasize Peter's role alone. Perhaps this shared leadership didn't fit with the narrative that later generations wanted to promote. Or perhaps Linus's contributions were overshadowed by Peter's martyrdom."

Marcus frowned. "But why Brythonic? Why bury these inscriptions in a language that most wouldn't be able to read, in such a hidden place?"

Michael shook his head, his mind racing through possibilities. "Perhaps Linus had followers among the early British Christians, or there was a group of believers connected to the Brythonic-speaking world who saw Linus's role as crucial to their understanding of Church leadership. It's unclear, but we know that Christianity spread early to Britain. This could be an early sign of that connection."

The silence between them grew heavy again as they both contemplated the enormity of what this inscription suggested.

Michael broke the silence, his voice firm but cautious. "We'll need to verify this, Marcus. If the inscription is authentic—and I believe it is—we have to tread carefully. This will certainly provoke questions, even challenges, to established doctrine about the origins of Church leadership."

Marcus nodded, understanding the gravity of what they were uncovering. "I'll bring in the necessary historians and epigraphists, but quietly. This stays between us until we know more."

Michael stood, crossing the room to look out the high window, the light fading as the evening deepened.

His hands were clasped behind his back, his mind still reeling. He was unnerved—deeply so—but also intrigued. The inscription felt like a missing piece of a puzzle that had never been fully revealed.

"I'll look into the archives tonight," Michael said softly, his voice barely audible over the growing darkness outside. "We need to understand what we've found before we decide how to proceed."

Marcus rose, closing his notebook carefully. "We're on the edge of something huge, Michael."

Michael nodded, but his expression was guarded, his thoughts still lingering on the words from the ancient stone. *Linus, brother to the rock.* The implications rippled through him like a slow, growing tide.

"Yes," he said, his voice low, "we are."

CHAPTER

TWENTY-SEVEN

The next day, Michael stood in the catacombs beneath the basilica, the soft hum of the Vatican's ancient stone walls almost comforting in their silence. Before him, the reliquary—crafted from sturdy, bulletproof glass—sat on a raised table. Inside, the nine tiny fragments of bone rested, each piece a testimony to the legacy of St. Peter. The bones glowed under the light, faint but distinct, like a quiet reminder of centuries of devotion.

Michael reached out, fingers brushing the cold surface of the glass. His touch lingered longer than necessary, his mind heavy with conflicting thoughts. This was no ordinary relic. These bones were the physical foundation upon which the Church itself was built—the rock, both literal and symbolic, of Peter's faith. And yet, as Michael gazed at them, a new weight pressed upon his conscience, a sense of responsibility that transcended even their spiritual significance. And he couldn't confuse this moment with the very real plight of the Peter-Linus situation. No, not yet.

The quiet shuffle of footsteps behind him interrupted his thoughts. Matteo Ferrante entered the room, his face set in the grave expression of someone handling something far beyond his lifetime.

"They're ready," Ferrante said quietly, nodding toward the reliquary. "No signs of wear. Everything seems… as expected."

Michael gave a slight nod, his eyes still fixed on the bones. "Good. I'll personally oversee the final placement."

Ferrante hesitated. "We've already been over the procedure, Father Dominic. The Swiss Guards are prepared. There's no need for you to—"

"I'll oversee it," Michael interrupted, his voice calm but firm. "No one else handles these. Not at this stage."

Ferrante blinked at him, taken aback by the uncharacteristic sternness. "Of course," he murmured, stepping back as Michael turned to face him fully.

For a long moment, neither spoke. Michael felt Ferrante's gaze on him, a silent question hanging in the air. Why was the prefect so insistent on these final steps? But Michael offered no explanation, merely gestured toward the door.

"I'll meet you in the exhibition tent shortly," Michael said. "But first, I want a few minutes alone with them."

Ferrante nodded again, still uncertain, but respectful of the priest's wishes. "As you wish, Father."

As soon as the door clicked shut behind Ferrante, Michael exhaled slowly. He turned back to the reliquary, his heartbeat quickening. Alone now, the thoughts that had been circling in his mind for days pressed closer.

He had been thinking of ways to protect the bones, of course. That was his duty, his sacred charge. But the threat wasn't just some external force trying to steal or desecrate them. No, the threat felt much closer—more intimate. Elliot Voss. His influence had woven itself into the Vatican's halls, subtle yet potent. He claimed to help, to fund the exhibition, but Michael sensed a deeper agenda, something that gnawed at him in the quiet hours of the night.

And now, with everything in place, Michael's instincts screamed at him. The bones were in danger, not just physically but symbolically. To lose them—to have them desecrated or used for some nefarious purpose— was unthinkable. But what could he do? Cancel the event? Alert the Vatican? Both options seemed out of reach, and time was running out.

He ran a hand over his face, feeling the weight of what was to come. His mind raced through the logistics. The public didn't need to know everything. Faith wasn't about the tangible—it was about the unseen, the eternal. People came to venerate St. Peter because of what he represented: steadfastness, faith, the foundation of the Church. The bones were sacred, but was their physical presence in the reliquary what truly mattered?

Michael's hand trembled slightly as he moved it away from the glass. He could hear Ferrante's voice from days ago: "The pilgrims come because they believe in something bigger than themselves, Father. This is their connection to the divine."

A pang of guilt shot through him as he recalled that conversation. Yes, the people came to connect with the divine. They sought hope, not the bones themselves but what they represented. And Michael knew, in the core of his being, that his duty wasn't just to protect the relics— it was to protect the faith they inspired.

Michael turned, his robes brushing against the cold stone floor as he moved toward the entrance. Outside, the Vatican was already alive with activity—pilgrims, guards, and the faithful all preparing for the exhibition. No one would question his decisions. No one would know the precautions he had taken.

But as he approached the door, he paused, casting one last glance at the reliquary behind him. The bones of St. Peter, sealed away, sacred, and silent. The faithful would still come. They would kneel, pray, weep, and venerate. But Michael knew that the truth—the real truth—was far more complex than they could ever imagine.

And as the door swung open, letting in a shaft of golden sunlight, Michael stepped out into the day, the burden of his choice weighing heavily on his soul.

TWENTY-EIGHT

elena Barrett's home lab was a stark contrast to the cool, ancient halls of the Vatican—a clinical, sterile space filled with the soft hum of modern equipment and the sharp, artificial light of overhead fixtures. Rows of meticulously organized shelves held various tools of her trade: high-powered magnifying lenses, syringes filled with chemical compounds, and delicate sculpting tools used to recreate the finest details of ancient artifacts. But tonight, the entire focus was on a single, ornately carved wooden box that sat open on the center of a stainless-steel workbench.

Helena stood back, her arms folded tightly across her chest, her eyes fixed on the box. She had spent countless hours replicating each fragment of St. Peter's bones, consulting every available source, public and private, every document, every high-resolution scan, and even the most obscure references from Vatican records Elliot Voss had somehow acquired for her. It had been her most complex, profitable—and dangerous— commission to date. And now it was done.

She stood over it, her fingers rapping nervously against the cool metal edge as she waited. Inside the box, cradled in a velvet lining of deep crimson, were the results of weeks of meticulous, painstaking work—nine bone fragments, perfectly replicated down to the tiniest detail, each one a nearly exact image of the relics she had been entrusted to recreate. Her heart pounded in her chest, a mix of exhilaration and dread, as she checked the position of each bone for the hundredth time, ensuring everything was flawless.

The sound of the lab's heavy door clicking open pulled her from her thoughts. She looked up just as Elliot Voss stepped inside, his presence filling the room with a palpable energy. He was dressed sharply, as always—his tailored suit immaculate, his expression one of barely contained excitement. He glanced around the lab briefly before his gaze settled on Helena and the open box before her.

"Helena," Voss said, his voice warm and eager, a broad smile spreading across his face. "I trust you have good news?"

She swallowed hard, feeling a brief flicker of unease that she quickly pushed aside. "I do," she said, trying to keep her voice steady. She gestured toward the box, her eyes locking onto Voss's as she stepped back to give him a better view. "It's all here. Everything you asked for."

Voss's eyes gleamed as he moved closer, his excitement barely restrained. He leaned over the workbench, his hands hovering just above the open box as if he were afraid to disturb the contents with even the slightest touch. The nine bone fragments lay there, their surfaces gleaming faintly in the lab's light, every detail precisely rendered—the tiny cracks, the patina of age, the faint traces of what appeared to be ancient wear.

"This is... remarkable," Voss murmured, his voice almost reverent. He reached out, his fingers grazing the edge of the ornate box, his gaze transfixed by the bones inside. "You've outdone yourself, Helena. Truly."

Helena allowed herself a brief, tight smile. She felt a surge of relief at his reaction. She had feared his scrutiny —Voss was nothing if not exacting, and she knew how high the stakes were. Her reputation, her fee, and perhaps more, hung in the balance. But as Voss's eyes roamed over the replicated bones, his expression shifted from cautious scrutiny to open admiration.

"Show me," he said, his voice dropping to a low, eager murmur. "Take me through each of them."

Helena nodded, slipping into her professional mode, the tension easing slightly as she began her presentation. She reached for two pairs of latex gloves, handing one pair to Voss. She pulled hers on with a practiced ease, and gently lifted the first bone from its velvet cradle—a slender fragment that bore the delicate marks of wear.

"This is the clavicle fragment," she said, holding it under the light so Voss could see the intricate details. "Notice the subtle irregularities in the surface texture. I replicated the micro-fractures using the samples you provided and combined them with what the official reports describe. Every angle, every line is accurate down to the sub-millimeter."

Voss leaned closer, his eyes narrowing as he examined the fragment, his face alight with an almost childlike wonder. "It's... perfect. Absolutely perfect."

Helena felt a swell of pride as she replaced the fragment and moved on to the next—another piece, larger, with a faint curve that suggested a rib. "This rib fragment was particularly difficult," she continued, her tone professional and controlled. "I had to simulate the exact mineral composition to match the originals. The patina was replicated with a multi-step process to ensure it wouldn't break down under different lighting conditions."

Voss nodded, barely hearing her, his attention focused entirely on the replica. He reached out and, with surprising gentleness, lifted the bone to study it for himself. A satisfied grin spread across his face as he returned it to the box. "It's incredible, Helena. Near as I can tell, you've captured the originals perfectly."

As they moved through each of the nine pieces, Helena's confidence grew. She spoke quickly, her explanations precise as she highlighted the technical aspects of her work—the fossilized coloration on a small fragment of femur, the smooth erosion marks on the edges of a phalange, the faint but crucial lines that mimicked centuries of handling. Voss listened intently, asking the occasional question but mostly remaining silent, absorbed in the examination of the bones.

Finally, they reached the last fragment—a small but vital piece that bore a faint, nearly imperceptible inscription that had only been recently detected on the original bone. Helena lifted it carefully, holding it just beneath the lab's magnifying light.

"This inscription," she said, her voice quieter now, "was the hardest to recreate. I had to blend ancient carving techniques with a modern chemical process to ensure it wouldn't be distinguishable, even under forensic examination."

Voss's eyes widened and he leaned in, scrutinizing the tiny, barely visible markings. He let out a slow breath, a smile spreading across his face as he glanced at her, admiration gleaming in his eyes. "You've thought of everything."

Helena's face remained impassive, but she felt the knot in her stomach relax just slightly. "I've done exactly what you requested," she said. "Every detail. Every specification. Note that all nine fragments are attached to their base by small but sturdy elastic cords, which themselves are bound to the back of the board on which all fragments rest. Which means, of course, that all fragments are handled as a single entity—exactly as the original bones are presented—bound to their base board, which is quite small, comparatively. So, if your plan is to replace the bones, you just have the presentation board to deal with rather than each bone individually."

Helena demonstrated, taking the final fragment from Voss's hands and securing it onto the base board inside the box with a black elastic cord designed to hold each bone fragment in place. "This makes it much easier to make the switch, rather than handle all nine pieces individually."

Voss straightened, turning to face her, his expression one of genuine gratitude. "You've exceeded my expectations, Helena. This is truly extraordinary work. You've done the impossible."

She nodded, accepting the praise with a small, professional smile. "I'm glad it meets your standards. Now, if you're satisfied, we can discuss the final fee."

"Of course, of course," Voss said quickly, a note of eagerness in his voice. He reached into his jacket pocket and pulled out a slim envelope, handing it to her with a flourish. "Your payment, as promised. And a little extra, for your discretion and the unparalleled quality of your craftsmanship."

Helena took the envelope, feeling the reassuring weight of a hefty cashier's check inside, and slipped it into her lab coat without a word. Voss's eyes lingered on her for a moment, his expression one of genuine appreciation and relief. He looked back at the ornate box, running a finger over the intricately carved lid.

"With these," he said softly, almost to himself, "I'll be able to proceed as planned. Everything will be in place for the exhibition."

He lifted the box with both hands, cradling it as though it contained the most precious treasure in the world. Helena watched him, a mixture of satisfaction and unease swirling inside her as he turned toward the door. Voss paused, glancing back at her with a broad smile.

"You've done me a great service, Helena. I won't forget this," he said.

She forced a smile in return, nodding as he left the lab, the heavy door swinging shut behind him. The moment he was gone, Helena's smile faded, replaced by a cold, empty feeling she couldn't quite name. She stood alone in the bright, sterile room, her eyes lingering on the empty space where the box had been.

It was done. The bones, real or not, were out of her hands.

TWENTY-NINE

The early October light spilled across St. Peter's Square, casting long, soft shadows as the Vatican personnel worked swiftly, preparing for the exhibition. The morning had a serene stillness, yet beneath it, there was a sense of urgency. Tomorrow, this vast expanse would be filled with thousands of pilgrims and visitors, their eyes fixed on the reliquary that would soon hold the sacred bones.

Michael stood near the edge of the square, watching as the transformation took place. Rows upon rows of chairs were being meticulously arranged, forming neat lines that stretched out across the cobbled ground surrounding the central Obelisk of Caligula, originally brought to Rome by Emperor Caligula in AD 37 from Heliopolis, Egypt. Workers moved efficiently, their voices low but steady as they coordinated the final stages of preparation. Barriers and cordons were carefully placed, ensuring that the flow of visitors would be orderly as they approached the centerpiece of the event—the bones exhibition tent.

From where Michael stood, the tent gleamed under the morning sun, its white canvas almost glowing against the backdrop of the basilica. It was grand yet understated, designed to hold the attention of thousands without distracting from the solemnity of what it would soon house. The reliquary table—still empty, its simplicity striking—was at the heart of it all, ready to bear its significant burden tomorrow. For now, though, it stood in quiet anticipation, its surface polished to a mirror-like sheen, reflecting the light filtering in through the tent flaps.

He began walking toward the tent. The sound of activity filled the square around him—more chairs being unloaded, barricades clicking into place, the soft murmur of Vatican staff conferring with one another. The preparations were moving like clockwork, each detail carefully considered, each step designed to ensure that everything would run flawlessly. The faithful would soon file into the square, tens of thousands of them, each hoping for a moment in the presence of the relics.

As Michael entered the tent, the cool air inside offered a brief respite from the sun outside. His eyes were immediately drawn to the empty table at its center. The simplicity of the setup struck him—the plain, elegant lines of the wooden table, its top partially lined with a luxuriant crimson cloth, perfectly positioned beneath the tent's soft lighting. Tomorrow, this would be the focal point, holding the reliquary that was already being guarded elsewhere, out of sight for now. But even without the bones, the space exuded a sense of reverence. The anticipation was palpable.

He moved closer, his footsteps echoing slightly on the polished floor. Two plainclothes Swiss Guards were nearby, adjusting the positions of the security cameras that had been discreetly installed throughout the tent. One guard stood at the back, fine-tuning a lens that was trained on the reliquary table itself, while another carefully checked the infrared sensors embedded into the surrounding area. Their movements were quiet, efficient, and nearly invisible to an untrained eye. But Michael saw them clearly—security was paramount here.

The table was immaculate, its smooth surface gleaming under the careful lighting. It looked almost like an altar, ready for the solemn ritual that would soon unfold. Michael allowed his fingers to hover just above the polished wood, his thoughts drifting for a moment. It was hard not to feel the weight of the occasion, even now, in the calm before everything began.

His gaze flicked up as more plainclothes guards entered the tent, their expressions focused, intent. They were checking everything—security cameras, motion detectors, every angle of the tent, ensuring that nothing was left unmonitored. The reliquary, once placed here tomorrow, would be under constant watch.

One of the guards approached Michael with a quick nod, offering a quiet update. "Everything is nearly set, Father Dominic. We'll do another sweep this evening before the final lockdown. The Swiss Guards will rotate in shifts once the event begins tomorrow."

Michael nodded, his attention briefly returning to the empty table. "Good. The crowd will be large—there's no room for mistakes."

The guard nodded once more before returning to his duties, leaving Michael standing alone in the center of the tent. He stood in silence for a moment, letting the calm wash over him, though his mind was anything but quiet. There was something about this moment—the quiet before the storm—that always carried an intensity of its own.

Outside the tent, the preparations continued at a brisk pace. The long queue lines were being laid out, stretching from the basilica's entrance and winding through the square, a labyrinth of barricades that would guide the faithful toward the tent. The workers moved with practiced precision, ensuring that every detail was perfect, every route clear.

Michael walked back toward the entrance of the tent, pausing just at the threshold. The sun had risen higher now, casting a brighter light across the square. He could see Monsignor Matteo Ferrante overseeing some final adjustments near the basilica steps, his expression focused, his gestures calm and controlled. Ferrante had been a constant presence throughout these preparations, ensuring that every aspect of the exhibition was seamless.

A breeze swept through the square, lifting the edges of the tent's canvas and bringing with it the sounds of the city beyond the Vatican's walls—faint, distant, but always present. Tomorrow, the quiet anticipation would be replaced with the hum of thousands of voices, the rustle of bodies moving forward in quiet reverence, the murmur of prayers carried on the wind.

Michael glanced back at the empty table, feeling the weight of the moment settle on him again. For now, the reliquary remained hidden, secure and unseen, but soon it would be the center of everything. He exhaled slowly, offering a quiet prayer for the days ahead—for the faithful who would come, for the sanctity of the event, for all that lay beyond his control.

CHAPTER

THIRTY

The morning sun cast a golden hue across St. Peter's Square, illuminating the massive crowd gathered for a day that would be etched into history. Thousands of pilgrims, their faces radiant with anticipation, filled the square, their murmurs blending into a low, reverent hum. Vatican flags fluttered in the breeze, and the faint strains of the Swiss Guard Band tuning their instruments carried through the air.

The majestic doors of St. Peter's Basilica opened slowly, revealing the beginning of the grand procession. A ripple of awe swept through the crowd as the Sistine Chapel Choir began to sing, their ethereal voices weaving a hymn that seemed to touch the heavens. The Swiss Guard Band followed, their brass and percussion instruments ringing out in solemn harmony, setting the rhythm for the steps of those who followed.

At the heart of the procession was Pope Clement,

resplendent in a white cassock adorned with gold embroidery, his tall miter glinting in the sunlight. His face, serene yet resolute, bore the weight of the occasion. Surrounding him were cardinals in vivid red robes, their caps and stoles reflecting the grandeur of the Church's traditions. Bishops, abbots, and other clergy formed part of the procession, their vestments shimmering in a kaleidoscope of gold, silver, and deep purple. The Swiss Guards flanked the pope, their halberds held high, their uniforms vibrant in red, blue, and yellow. Behind them marched the full Swiss Guard Band, their disciplined formation amplifying the power of the music.

As the procession moved forward, a palpable wave of emotion swept through the crowd. Pilgrims knelt in prayer; others wept openly. Cameras flashed, though none could fully capture the spiritual weight of the moment. The choir's voices rose higher, joined by the triumphant strains of the band, as Pope Clement and his entourage reached a temporary outdoor altar constructed near the front of the square.

The altar, a masterpiece of Vatican artistry, was covered in crimson-and-gold cloth, with ornate carvings of angelic figures adorning its sides. Behind it stood an imposing reliquary, sealed in bulletproof glass, resting on a pedestal draped in white silk. Within the reliquary lay the fragments of bone—nine pieces that tradition held were the mortal remains of St. Peter himself.

The pope climbed the steps to the altar, pausing at the top to spread his arms in a gesture of blessing over the crowd. His voice, amplified by discreetly placed microphones, carried across the square as he began a prayer in Latin, invoking the spirit of the first apostle and asking for divine intercession to guide the Church in troubled times.

"*Sancte Petre, Apostole Christi, ora pro nobis,*" he intoned, his voice rich and resonant. The crowd echoed the words, their voices united in devotion.

A cardinal approached the reliquary, holding a golden aspergillum filled with holy water. He handed it reverently to the pope, who took it and began to bless the relics, sprinkling the holy water over the glass with slow, deliberate motions. Incense rose in curls from censers held by altar servers, filling the air with a rich, smoky aroma that mingled with the prayers and hymns.

As Pope Clement concluded the blessing, he placed his hand briefly on the glass of the reliquary, his face lined with deep reflection. Then, turning back to the crowd, he spoke, his voice filled with both authority and compassion.

"Today, we honor the foundation of our Church," he said, addressing the sea of faces before him. "St. Peter, the rock upon whom Christ built His Church, stands with us still, through these sacred relics and through the faith that lives in each of us. May this day renew our commitment to the Gospel and to the unity of our global family."

The applause that followed was thunderous, a wave of sound that echoed against the towering columns of the basilica. As the pope stepped away from the altar, attendants carefully wheeled the reliquary down the steps, guided by Swiss Guards and clergy. The glass enclosure gleamed in the sunlight, mesmerizing the crowd as it was carried into the specially constructed exhibition tent nearby.

The tent itself was a marvel—a temporary yet grand structure made of pristine white fabric and reinforced with gold-trimmed columns. Inside, soft lighting illuminated the reliquary, enhancing its sacred aura. The pope, accompanied by his entourage, entered first, offering a final prayer before stepping aside to allow the faithful their turn.

Outside, Vatican officials began organizing the queue, inviting the crowd to approach in reverence and silence. Pilgrims shuffled forward, many clutching rosaries or small gifts to leave at the base of the reliquary. Some wept as they neared the relics, while others knelt in awe, their prayers whispered under their breath.

The Sistine Chapel Choir continued their hymns, their voices blending seamlessly with the Swiss Guard Band's music. The sound spilled out into the square, creating an atmosphere of deep solemnity and joy.

For hours, the faithful streamed through the tent; each person granted a moment to gaze upon the relics of the first apostle. The air was thick with incense and devotion, a living testament to the enduring power of faith. In this moment, the centuries seemed to collapse, connecting the modern Church to its ancient beginnings, all through the presence of nine fragments of bone that had witnessed the birth of a spiritual legacy.

And at the heart of it all, as the sun began to set behind the basilica's dome, the pope stood quietly to one side, his face calm and contemplative. Today wasn't merely an exhibition—it was a reaffirmation of everything the Church stood for, a day that had drawn the faithful closer to the divine through the relics of St. Peter and the enduring message of love and unity they represented.

CHAPTER
THIRTY-ONE

The next day, morning sun filtered softly through the tent's walls, casting a warm, golden glow over the reliquary where the fragments of St. Peter's bones lay displayed beneath the glass. A gentle thrum of reverence filled the air, as a steady stream of pilgrims began to enter, eyes wide with awe, hands folded in prayer. The first group slowly approached the reliquary, their steps tentative, as if they were afraid to break the sacred silence that had settled over the space.

Michael stood at a distance, close to the tent's entrance. His arms were folded beneath his cassock, his face impassive. From where he stood, he could observe everything yet remain unnoticed. His eyes followed the movement of the pilgrims, their heads bowed, their hands trembling as they knelt before the reliquary. The quiet murmurs of prayer floated up, soft and indistinct, mixing with the faint rustle of robes and the shuffle of feet.

A family—mother, father, and two small children—had reached the front. The father, his eyes wet with emotion, placed a hand on his son's shoulder as they knelt together. The little girl, no more than six or seven, pressed her palms together in prayer, her lips moving in silent reverence. Her wide, innocent eyes fixed on the bones, her face glowing with a simple, unquestioning faith.

Michael's gaze lingered on the girl, her quiet devotion stirring something deep within him. He took in a slow breath, steadying himself. Witnessing such pure belief and unshakable trust in the divine was always humbling. These people had traveled great distances to be here, to kneel before what were believed to be the remains of the first pope, the apostle who had laid the foundation of the Church.

His hands tightened in the folds of his robes. They believed, and that was enough. Their faith wouldn't be shaken by what they couldn't know. The bones, after all, were a symbol—a link to something much greater than the fragments encased in the glass. And as he watched the family rise, the father wiping a tear from his eye, Michael felt a quiet sense of satisfaction. He had done what was necessary to protect the sanctity of the relics, to ensure that they would remain untarnished by greed or malice.

The next group of pilgrims moved forward—an elderly woman, supported by her son, shuffled slowly to the front. Her hands trembled as she reached out to touch the glass, her fingers brushing the surface as though she could feel the holiness radiating from within. Her son stood close beside her, steadying her frail frame, his own head bowed in prayer.

Michael's chest tightened slightly as he watched her. She was old, her body frail, her steps uncertain, but her faith was unwavering. There was no question in her mind—no doubt as to what lay beneath the glass. For her, this was a moment of profound connection to the divine, a culmination of years, perhaps decades, of devotion. The quiet intensity of her belief struck him in a way that made him pause, just for a moment.

His lips moved in a prayer of his own, barely audible. "Grant them Your grace, Lord." The words felt natural, instinctive, a part of the rhythm of the day.

As the woman slowly rose with her son's help, a sense of calm returned to Michael. The exhibition was unfolding as expected. The pilgrims' devotion was deep, sincere, and undisturbed by any hint of doubt. He had ensured that the relics were safe, and the faithful were receiving what they had come for—something larger than any one fragment, something eternal.

Another group entered the tent—more families, pilgrims, and prayers. Each face, each bowed head, carried with it the same quiet reverence. Michael allowed himself to relax slightly. The faithful weren't here to scrutinize the bones. They were here for something far greater, something that transcended the physical. The relics were a vessel for that faith, nothing more.

He glanced toward the reliquary, watching as more

hands touched the glass, eyes filled with tears, and voices whispered in prayer. These moments belonged to the faithful, to their personal connection with the divine. The bones, whether seen or unseen, were part of that connection.

Michael remained in the background, his presence unnoticed, as the line of pilgrims continued on into the evening. A quiet, steady devotion flowed through the space, undisturbed by anything else. The prayers rose, carried by the warmth of the tent's lighting, and Michael, his hands folded tightly beneath his robes, whispered one final prayer of his own.

"Let their faith be unshaken."

And in the stillness, he found himself reassured—not by the bones, not by the reliquary, but by the enduring power of the faith that filled the room.

THIRTY-TWO

On the third evening of the exhibition, Karl Dengler and Lukas Bischoff stood like sentinels on either side of the relic table, their imposing figures framed by the soft glow of the tent's lighting. Their presence was a study in contrasts: the ceremonial gleam of their polished armor spoke to a centuries-old tradition, but the intensity in their eyes betrayed the modern, elite training that had earned them their positions among the Swiss Guards.

Karl, broad-shouldered and steady, exuded a quiet, almost intimidating calm, his gaze scanning the crowd with the precision of a marksman. Lukas, leaner but no less formidable, carried a coiled energy that made his watchfulness seem almost predatory. Together, they were an unspoken bulwark, their disciplined stances a silent warning to any who might think to cross the line from reverence to malice.

Though they stood motionless, their minds were far

from still. Karl's sharp eyes followed subtle movements —a hand lingering too long near a camera strap, a figure shifting nervously in the queue. Lukas's attention flicked between faces, reading microexpressions and cataloging anything that struck him as unusual. Every moment was a calculation, a judgment, an anticipation of what might happen before it did.

They both knew the stakes. These bones were more than relics; they were a symbol of faith, a connection to the Church's foundation. Yet, they were also a prize for those who saw them only as artifacts of immense historical and monetary value. The whispers of potential threats, the rumors of plots, hung in their minds like shadows, and neither man would allow complacency to put this sacred moment at risk.

Karl shifted his weight slightly, his gauntlet-clad hand resting on the hilt of his ceremonial sword—a gesture that to the untrained eye seemed formal but to Lukas signaled readiness. Without a word, Lukas mirrored the subtle movement, their years of training and trust rendering communication unnecessary. Together, they were more than guards; they were protectors of something far greater than themselves.

The crowd flowed past, some murmuring prayers, others staring in silent awe at the glass-encased relics. Karl and Lukas remained watchful, their disciplined presence a reminder that holiness was not exempt from danger—and that these two men stood as the final barrier between the sacred and the profane.

In the back of the tent, standing apart from the crowd, Elliot Voss observed it all with cool, detached focus. To anyone watching, he was merely another visitor, a figure of quiet respect amid the sea of pilgrims, though the Swiss Guards knew he was a prominent coordinator of the event, knowing to allow him free movement around the relics. His expression was calm, almost serene, but beneath that composed exterior, a relentless calculation ticked away. This moment had been in the making for months. The planning, the patience, the subtle manipulations—it all led to this singular moment.

The faithful continued to shuffle past the reliquary, pausing to bow, murmur prayers, or simply gaze at the fragments with wide-eyed devotion. Voss, however, wasn't interested in the piety of the crowd. His gaze flicked briefly toward the two Swiss Guards as he slowly made his way toward the table. Their discipline was impeccable, and they showed no signs of fatigue. But Voss wasn't relying on human error. His way in wasn't through brute force or a clumsy distraction. It was through something far more reliable: protocols.

The timing, as always, was everything.

The guards had been standing watch for nearly two hours now, and Voss had timed every part of his operation to match the precise shift change. In five minutes, at 8:00 p.m. sharp, these guards would be replaced by another pair, fresh and equally disciplined. This was when the first part of his plan would unfold— when the Vatican's well-oiled machinery would, for just a few brief moments, be vulnerable.

The shift change would occur in perfect synchrony with a subtle, planned malfunction. For weeks, Voss had used his contacts, manipulating the city's infrastructure, to ensure that a minor power grid disruption would strike the Vatican's lighting and surveillance system—just enough to cause a flicker in the cameras, just enough to cause a five-minute blackout.

At the precise moment, the lights inside the tent flickered once, then twice, before plunging the space into brief darkness. A low murmur spread through the crowd, the sudden shift in atmosphere unsettling the faithful. Some of them gasped quietly, clutching rosaries or crossing themselves. Vatican staff moved swiftly to reassure the crowd, their voices rising in gentle reassurance, telling them the lights would return in moments.

The Swiss Guards, ever the professionals, remained in their positions, their forms rigid and unyielding. Yet Voss knew that even their training had limits. In those brief seconds of darkness, their instinct would be to tense, to scan for danger, to anticipate the unknown. And that was when hesitation—just a whisper of doubt —would creep in.

Voss moved with precision, slipping forward just as planned. His steps were silent, his body language unassuming, blending with the nervous rustling of the crowd. The guards, momentarily disoriented by the darkness, exchanged a brief glance—subtle, but there. Just enough to divide their attention. They couldn't see the crowd, and they couldn't risk moving, not until the situation clarified itself.

At that exact moment, a carefully orchestrated distraction unfolded. One of Voss's accomplices, a young woman posing as a tourist, stumbled deliberately in the dark near the entrance to the tent. Her bag hit the ground with a loud thud, scattering its contents across the floor. She gasped, her voice ringing out in feigned surprise as she fumbled to gather her belongings.

Both Swiss Guards instinctively turned toward the sound, their eyes narrowing as they assessed the situation. The moment of confusion was brief, but it was all Voss needed.

In the cover of the darkened tent, with the crowd still distracted by the sudden malfunction and the guards momentarily diverted, Voss acted. Hidden in the sleeve of his jacket was a device no larger than a fountain pen. He had obtained it from a contact in Zurich—an expert in electronic locks and surveillance systems. The device emitted a frequency pulse designed to momentarily disrupt the electronic lock that secured the bulletproof glass over the reliquary.

He pressed the device against the glass with a slight motion, and the pulse did its job. No alarms, no sound, just a faint vibration in his hand as the lock disengaged. The lid was now accessible.

Voss's fingers moved quickly, lifting the glass lid with the precision of a surgeon. From a specially sewn compartment hidden in his jacket, he produced the red velvet base board containing the nine replica bones, each crafted with meticulous care by Helena Barrett.

He swapped the replicas for the original bones, his movements swift but deliberate. The genuine fragments on their original red velvet board, now hidden in the same compartment in his jacket, felt heavy against his chest—a gravity of legacy that no one in the crowd would realize had just been stolen.

The guards shifted again, sensing that the blackout was about to end. Voss placed the glass lid back into place with the same care, the device in his hand sending one final pulse to reactivate the lock. The click of the lock engaging was barely audible, lost in the nervous murmur of the crowd.

Moments later, the lights flickered back on, bathing the tent in warm light once again. The cameras resumed their feed, and the Swiss Guards, now back in full control, straightened as the scene returned to normal. No one—not the guards, not the crowd, not even the Vatican staff—had noticed a thing.

The young woman at the entrance finished gathering her things, offering embarrassed apologies as she moved away, her role in the diversion complete. Voss stood there, his hands clasped behind his back, his face an expression of quiet reverence.

The guards, oblivious to the change that had occurred in the few minutes of darkness, resumed their watch. Their replacements arrived on schedule, and the shift change occurred without a hitch. But the original bones—the fragments that had rested in the reliquary for all to see—were now safely hidden inside Elliot Voss's jacket.

Voss moved through the crowd as they filed out of the tent, his heart steady, his movements calm. His plan had worked flawlessly, the culmination of months of preparation coming to fruition in a matter of minutes.

He had done it—he had switched the bones, setting the stage for the next phase.

As he stepped out into the Roman night, the weight of the relics against his chest felt both exhilarating and dangerous. The real bones were his now, and the world had no idea what had just taken place beneath the shadow of St. Peter's Basilica. His steps were measured, purposeful, as he disappeared into the crowd, leaving behind the unsuspecting eyes of the Vatican, the Swiss Guards, and the faithful.

CHAPTER
THIRTY-THREE

As the night wore on, the soft murmur of prayers continued to echo through the tent as the faithful moved slowly, reverently, toward the reliquary. The atmosphere was heavy with devotion, the low whispers of prayer mixing with the quiet shuffle of feet on the stone floor. Pilgrims knelt before the glass case, heads bowed, their eyes filled with reverence as they gazed at what their faith informed them were the sacred bones of St. Peter. From his vantage point near the entrance, Father Michael Dominic observed the flow of people with satisfaction.

As he moved through the huge tent, offering quiet blessings to the faithful, Michael found himself drawn toward the reliquary at the center once again. It gleamed under the soft lighting, the nine bone fragments nestled in their red velvet bed, perfectly arranged. He had spent hours inspecting them before they were placed inside the glass case, ensuring every detail was just right. Yet now, as he approached the display, a strange feeling of unease washed over him.

He stepped closer to the reliquary, his eyes narrowing as he studied the bones. The faithful continued to pass by him, unaware of his growing tension, their prayers rising softly in the air. At first glance, the bones looked unchanged—exactly as they had when they were placed in the case. But something was wrong. Michael's breath caught as he leaned in, his heart suddenly pounding in his chest.

The bones... they weren't the same.

A chill ran through him as he scanned the fragments more closely, his mind racing. He knew these bones. He had studied them intimately, committed every fracture, every weathered line to memory. And now, standing there, he could see it—subtle differences. The texture was off, the patina too uniform, the wear too pristine. These weren't the bones that had been placed inside the reliquary earlier. His heart sank as the full weight of realization hit him.

The bones had been swapped.

Michael stood frozen, his hand hovering over the glass, his mind reeling as he tried to piece together what had happened. He glanced around, his eyes darting to the Swiss Guards standing at attention, then to the faithful moving slowly through the tent, oblivious to what had occurred. His pulse quickened, and his mind raced through the day's events.

The blackout.

It had been brief—lights out for barely a couple of minutes. At the time, it seemed like nothing more than a technical glitch, a momentary hiccup in the smooth execution of the exhibition. But now, Michael saw it for what it was: a perfect opportunity for someone to have accessed the reliquary without drawing attention. Whoever had swapped the bones had done so during that blackout.

His chest tightened as he thought about the security cameras. The cameras had been running non-stop, installed at every corner of the tent, monitoring the reliquary from every angle. There would be footage. He could trace exactly what happened, identify who had been near the case during those crucial moments.

As he turned to head for the control room, something else clicked in his mind—a memory from just before the blackout. *Voss.*

Elliot Voss had been lingering near the Swiss Guards earlier, making polite conversation, his sharp eyes scanning the tent as if taking in every detail. Michael hadn't thought much of it at the time—Voss had been involved in the planning of the exhibition, after all—but now, it felt significant. Too significant. Voss had been right there, moments before the blackout, chatting with the guards just as the lights flickered out.

Michael's stomach twisted with a cold realization. *It had to be him.* Voss had orchestrated the blackout. He had used the chaos and confusion to switch the bones, inserting his own replicas into the reliquary. The thought made Michael's blood run cold. How had Voss managed it? And more importantly, why?

The weight of it all pressed down on him as he made

his way quickly through the tent. He had to get to the control room. He had to see the footage for himself.

Reaching the security hub, Michael stepped inside the small room. The hum of monitors filled the air, and several technicians sat at their stations, keeping a watchful eye on the live feeds from the cameras in the tent. He approached the nearest technician, his voice low and urgent.

"Please pull up the footage from the blackout," he urged. "I need to see everything that happened near the reliquary during that time."

The technician glanced at him, a flicker of surprise crossing his face, but he nodded quickly and began navigating through the stored video. The tension in the room grew thick as the screen flickered, rewinding back to the moment the lights had gone out. Michael's heart pounded in his chest as he leaned in, eyes glued to the screen.

The footage was eerie in its simplicity. The lights flickered, and for a few seconds, the cameras went dark. Then, just as quickly as it had begun, the blackout ended. Michael's eyes narrowed as the feed resumed, showing the moments immediately after the lights returned. His gaze fixed on the figure standing just beyond the reliquary, near the Swiss Guards.

Voss.

There he was, standing calmly as if nothing had happened. But Michael's eyes sharpened, scanning the flicker of movement during the brief blackout. A shadow—a figure near the table. It was subtle, almost imperceptible, but there it was. When the lights came back on, everything appeared normal, but Michael knew better.

Voss was the only one in proximity. His calm demeanor, his timing—it all pointed to him.

Michael's fists clenched, his jaw tightening as anger simmered beneath his calm exterior. Voss had been planning this for who knew how long, waiting for the perfect moment to make his move. And now he had swapped the bones right under everyone's noses.

But there was still time. Michael could still expose him.

Turning back to the technician, Michael's voice was steady but firm. "Keep watching the footage. I want every angle, every detail. We need to know exactly who else was suspicious during the blackout, if anyone."

The technician nodded, eyes wide with focus as he continued combing through the footage. Michael turned and left the control room, his mind racing with a plan. Voss had made his move, but Michael wasn't about to let him get away with it.

He would confront Voss, find out where the original bones on display had gone, and uncover the full extent of the plot. And when the time came, Voss would answer for what he had done.

But for now, a sly smile crossed Michael's face as he moved swiftly through the tent, determined to stay one more step ahead.

THIRTY-FOUR

Elliot Voss moved swiftly through the narrow corridors of the Vatican, the hum of the exhibition still pulsing in the distance. His heart pounded with an electric sense of accomplishment, his steps brisk, purposeful. The switch had gone flawlessly. The bones were now in his possession, and no one suspected a thing—at least not yet. Even if it were to be detected somehow, by then, Voss would be long gone.

Emerging from the side entrance that led to a restricted area of St. Peter's Square, Voss caught a glimpse of the faithful still queuing outside the exhibition tent, unaware of the deception that had unfolded mere meters from them. He allowed himself a brief smile, a mix of satisfaction and exhilaration washing over him. All the meticulous planning, the careful execution—it had paid off. He had pulled off the impossible right under the Vatican's nose.

His sleek black Mercedes S-Class sedan was already waiting at the exit, the driver standing by, opening the door for him with a respectful nod. Voss slid into the leather seat, pulling the door shut behind him. The cool interior of the car was a welcome respite from the tension that had surrounded him at the Vatican. He exhaled deeply, sinking back into the seat as the car pulled away from the cobblestones of the ancient square.

"Fiumicino, please," he said to the driver, his voice calm now, the adrenaline slowly receding. The drive to Rome's international airport wouldn't take long, and Voss's private jet was already prepped and waiting at the Signature terminal.

As the car moved through the dark, winding streets of Rome, Voss's mind drifted to what awaited him in Seattle—his private museum, tucked away in the expansive grounds of his estate, where the world's rarest artifacts, many stolen or bought through shadowy deals, were housed. The thought of adding some of St. Peter's bones to that collection made his pulse quicken again. This would be the crown jewel. For years, Voss had amassed relics and artifacts of immense historical significance, but none compared to these. Yet there was so much more with this particular relic. The most viable of the bones would be used in his laboratory to work on his lifelong project: the source of DNA that would provide immortality. The once-only-imagined possibility of immortality would be in his hands at last. He had no doubt that the key to heaven as promised in numerous sources to be found through St. Peter meant the key to eternal life. What else could be closer to heaven?

The car pulled up to the private Signature terminal at Fiumicino, bypassing the crowds of tourists and travelers. Voss stepped out, not bothering to glance at the regular passengers streaming into the main terminal. For him, airports weren't places of waiting and lines— they were mere gateways to wherever he needed to go, with no delays, no checks.

As he walked briskly toward the jet, the wind from the engines tousling his hair, he felt a surge of excitement. His pilot was already at the helm, the plane idling on the tarmac, waiting only for him to board. He climbed the stairs, the weight of the moment settling on him again as the door hissed shut behind him.

Inside the luxurious cabin, Voss moved to the small, ornate box he had stowed when leaving Seattle, cradled in a padded compartment in the overhead storage. He removed the display board containing the bones from his jacket pocket and inserted it into the box. With a smile, he closed the glass top.

"Are you comfortable, Mr. Voss?" the flight attendant asked softly, offering him a drink.

"Perfectly," he replied, barely glancing at her as he fastened his seatbelt.

The engines roared to life within minutes, and the jet taxied down the runway. Voss gazed out the window as Rome began to fade into the distance, the ancient city shrinking beneath him. He felt untouchable, beyond reach. By the time anyone at the Vatican realized what had happened, he would be halfway across the Atlantic.

As the jet leveled out, cruising high above the clouds, Voss gazed down at the bones again, his eyes gleaming with satisfaction. Each fragment was carefully cushioned in its velvet lining, each with the aged markings he had demanded from Barrett to be shown on the replicas.

In his mind, these weren't just relics of a saint. They were trophies, proof that he had outwitted the most powerful institution on Earth. He had taken something priceless, not just in monetary value but also in spiritual and historical significance, and made it his own. The Church believed it was the custodian of history, but now, the most precious part of that history belonged to him.

Voss imagined the bones displayed in his private museum, the centerpiece of his collection. Only a select few would ever know, even fewer would ever see it, but that didn't matter to him. The knowledge that he had done it—had taken what was thought untouchable— was all the satisfaction he needed. And, in time, when his quest for immortality also played out using the key DNA from these bones, he would have eternity to add to his claims on history.

The flight passed in a haze of contentment. As the hours slipped by, Voss allowed himself to drift into thoughts of the future. With the Vatican none the wiser, he would soon be back in Seattle, back in his secluded mansion where the world couldn't touch him.

~

By the time the jet began its descent toward Seattle, night had fallen across the Pacific Northwest. The sprawling lights of the city glittered far below, but Voss's estate was beyond the city, nestled in the private hills outside the bustling metropolis. The jet touched down smoothly, and Voss felt the familiar satisfaction of being back on his own turf, back where he held all the cards.

As he stepped off the jet and into the crisp night air, his Tesla Model S Stretch Limousine was already waiting. The driver carefully loaded the small box into the back, and soon, they were on their way, winding through the freeways and darkened roads toward his estate.

A bit later, the iron gates of his mansion loomed ahead, swinging open as they approached. Voss felt a surge of triumph as they drove up the long, winding driveway lined with manicured trees and the occasional discreet security post. He had arrived.

Once inside, Voss wasted no time. He carried the box himself, walking through the grand halls of his home, past priceless paintings and sculptures, until he reached the private wing where his museum lay hidden. The heavy door swung open under his hand, and he stepped inside the dimly lit room that housed his collection.

The room was a labyrinth of glass cases and shadowed alcoves, each display carefully curated to house treasures from around the world—rare manuscripts, ancient coins, religious relics. But now, at the center, would sit his greatest prize.

Voss placed the box on a pedestal, his fingers

lingering on the lock as he undid the latch. Slowly, reverently, he opened the lid, and for the first time since the bones had come into his possession, he allowed himself to simply stare.

The bones of the first Apostle, St. Peter.

A smile crept across his face, slow and satisfied. He had done it.

The Vatican had no idea what it had lost.

THIRTY-FIVE

Michael paced through the halls of the Vatican, his mind racing. Every corridor he searched, every room he passed through—Voss was nowhere to be found. It was as if he had vanished into thin air. Michael had tried calling him multiple times, but each call went unanswered. A sinking feeling had settled deep in his stomach, the truth becoming clearer with every passing minute: Voss was gone.

He paused near a side exit leading into the quiet gardens, pulling out his phone once more. Staring at the screen, he dialed Voss's number again. His heart pounded in his chest as the call rang and rang, only to go to voicemail. He clenched his jaw, his fingers tightening around the phone.

He's already gone. He's probably on his way back to Seattle. The thought hit him like a cold wave. Voss had done it—pulled off the switch, left without a trace, and now was undoubtedly airborne, the stolen bones likely already secured in his possession.

Michael leaned against the stone wall of the Vatican Gardens, closing his eyes for a moment. The weight of the situation pressed down on him, but the realization that chasing Voss now would be fruitless washed over him. There would be no stopping him before he landed in Seattle. The chase would have to wait. There were steps to take here first, and Michael couldn't afford to unravel yet. Not now.

He exhaled slowly, his mind shifting. He needed to regroup, to think clearly, and to plan his next move carefully. And right now, that meant stepping away from the intensity of the day. As his thoughts settled, another person came to mind—Hana. She had been working on her own story, keeping her distance from the exhibition so far, but Michael had always found her presence steadying, her sharp instincts a perfect complement to his.

Without hesitation, he dialed her number.

The phone rang only once before Hana picked up. "Hana, I…" He paused.

"Michael? Is everything all right?" Her voice was familiar, comforting, though laced with concern. He could imagine her sitting somewhere with her notebook or laptop, always ready to dive into the next story, always alert to the undercurrents of any situation. And the undercurrents of his voice.

He forced his voice to remain steady. "It's been a day, to put it mildly. I could use a break. Are you free for dinner now?"

There was a brief silence on the other end of the line. Michael could almost hear her processing the invitation, her journalist's instincts likely pricking up at the tone in his voice. She didn't press, though, for which Michael was grateful.

"I'm free," she said, her voice softening slightly. "Where are we meeting?"

Relief washed over him, and a small smile tugged at the corner of his lips, despite the tension still gripping his mind. "How about Caffè Pergamino? It's quiet, and I could use some time away from the Vatican."

Hana let out a light chuckle. "That sounds perfect. I'll meet you there in thirty minutes?"

Michael glanced at his watch. Thirty minutes felt like just enough time to leave the weight of the Vatican behind, even if temporarily. "See you then."

He hung up, pocketing his phone. The cold air of the gardens felt sharper against his skin now, as if the weight of what had just transpired—the failure to stop Voss—was sinking deeper. But knowing he was going to see Hana eased the pressure, if only slightly. He could breathe again, and he needed that more than anything at the moment.

THIRTY MINUTES LATER, Michael arrived at Caffè Pergamino, the familiar scent of coffee and soft candlelight spilling out from the cozy interior. The small café was nestled on a quiet side street, far from the crowds of tourists and the noise of the Vatican. It had become something of a retreat for him—a place to escape, to think, and to speak freely without the weight of history pressing down on him.

As he stepped inside, the warmth of the café enveloped him, a welcome contrast to the cold tension of the day. Hana was already there, seated at a corner table by the window, her notebook open in front of her. She looked up as he approached, a smile flickering across her face, though her eyes held the questions she hadn't yet asked.

"Michael," she said as he sat down across from her. "You do look like you've had a rough day."

He chuckled softly, rubbing the back of his neck. "You could say that."

Hana closed her notebook and leaned forward slightly, her gaze softening as she studied him. "You're not going to tell me everything yet, are you?"

Michael smiled, but his eyes didn't quite shown it. "Not tonight," he admitted. "There's too much to unpack, and I need time to figure out the next steps. But I needed to get away for a bit. I thought dinner with you might help clear my head."

She raised an eyebrow, clearly intrigued, but didn't push. Instead, she gestured toward the menu sitting between them. "Well, then, let's start with dinner. And maybe afterward, you can tell me whatever you can share."

Michael nodded, grateful for her understanding. He scanned the menu absently, his mind still tangled in the web of thoughts about Voss and the stolen bones. But as the evening wore on, with the clink of silverware and the murmur of low conversation surrounding them, he began to feel some of the weight lift. Being here, with Hana, allowed him to push the chaos to the background, even if just for a little while.

The conversation drifted, light and comfortable, and for the first time that day, Michael felt a sliver of calm return. The Vatican, the bones, the Peter-Linus issue, and the mystery of Voss could wait until tomorrow.

For tonight, he was content to sit with Hana, let the evening unfold, and remember that there was still time to right the wrongs ahead.

CHAPTER
THIRTY-SIX

I n the recessed glow of his private museum, Elliot
Voss slowly opened the lid, revealing the
fragments resting on red velvet. The air seemed to
thicken around him as he reached inside, lifting one of
the bones with steady hands. He turned it over carefully,
feeling the weight of centuries pressing into his palm.
This was the beginning. From here, he would set in
motion the meticulous process to extract whatever
sacred energy might linger within these ancient relics,
bending it to serve his vision of endless life.

He carried the bone to a sleek lab table positioned
against the far wall, where state-of-the-art scientific
equipment stood in sharp contrast to the ancient artifact
in his hand. Each device was selected for its precision,
custom-designed for this purpose. He began by setting
the fragment under a high-powered microscope, the
lenses illuminating it in stark clarity. Every groove,
every imperfection and discoloration was revealed with

perfect precision. Voss's gloved hand moved delicately as he adjusted the controls, his breath catching as the bone revealed its microscopic structure.

In theory, the bones held no more power than any other ancient relic, but Voss's research hinted at the possibility of something extraordinary, hidden in the very marrow of the apostle's remains. He leaned closer, a faint smile playing on his lips as he observed the mineralized structure that had withstood the ravages of time. If these fragments held even a trace of Peter's essence—of the conviction and resilience of the first follower—then they might indeed possess the key to life itself.

He turned to a small glass vial containing a deep blue liquid, a compound his team had developed to extract DNA from even the most ancient remains. He lifted it, studying the liquid for a moment, marveling at the scientific achievement it represented. This wasn't the work of alchemists, but of geneticists and biochemists who had spent years perfecting its formula under his direction. He would use this compound to unlock whatever hidden genetic secrets might remain within the bones, secrets that had been buried for millennia.

"Let's begin," he murmured to himself, his voice echoing softly in the quiet of the room.

With careful precision, Voss lowered the bone fragment into a small glass dish and using a delicate dropper, he added a single drop of the extraction compound. The liquid spread across the surface of the bone, seeping into every microscopic crevice. He watched closely, his heartbeat accelerating as the bone absorbed the compound. This was the first step—the gentle unlocking of whatever ancient remnants lay embedded within.

As the minutes passed, Voss found himself transfixed, his mind racing with visions of what could come next. The possibilities were boundless. With these bones, he would construct a foundation for human evolution that defied death itself. He would reprogram the essence of humanity, incorporating these secrets into his own DNA, and—eventually—into those who might pay to be his followers, disciples in a new age where death would be nothing but a shadow from the past.

He removed the bone from the dish, holding it reverently in his hands, and examined it once more. There would be further stages to this process: sequencing, integration, testing—each step carefully designed to prevent decay of the material and maximize whatever faint genetic echoes of Peter's essence remained. But this first step was complete.

He looked around at the room filled with relics. Every artifact spoke of the history he now meant to rewrite: scrolls chronicling the rise and fall of empires, fragments of martyrdom and faith, icons of lives cut short by time and mortality. But not anymore. Voss would transcend those limits. He would become the culmination of their hopes and ambitions, the eternal figure they had dreamed of but never achieved.

And yet, as he looked down at the bones, a faint shadow of doubt flickered in the back of his mind. He remembered Icarus and Pandora, reminders of humanity's fraught relationship with ambition. Each had pursued the extraordinary, only to find themselves destroyed by their desires. History's cautionary tales whispered at the edges of his thoughts, but Voss pushed them aside, steeling himself.

This was different. This was the apex of science and ambition, perfected. He wasn't bound by superstition or myth. He was backed by the unshakable foundation of knowledge, driven by the ceaseless advancement of technology.

Voss took a slow, deliberate breath, his hand tightening around the bone as if he could feel the potential pulsing within it. He would show the world that faith, science, and human will could come together to forge something undying. And in doing so, he would carve his name into history, transcending all who had come before him.

With renewed determination, he placed the bone back into the box, shutting the lid with a quiet, resolute click. This was only the beginning.

As Voss sealed the box, a soft chime echoed through the museum. His eyes darted to the security monitor mounted discreetly in the corner. A figure moved through the shadowy corridors of the downstairs laboratory, approaching the museum's entrance. He recognized the silhouette instantly—Dr. Amelia Chen, his lead geneticist.

Voss's jaw tightened. He hadn't summoned her, and her unexpected presence threatened to disrupt the delicate balance of secrecy he had cultivated. With swift, practiced movements, he secured the bone fragments and activated the room's state-of-the-art air filtration system, erasing any trace of his experiments.

Once satisfied he had secured the room, Voss actuated the entrance lock. The door slid open with a pneumatic hiss, revealing Dr. Chen's lithe form. Her dark eyes, usually sharp with scientific curiosity, now held a hint of apprehension. The scent of jasmine and antiseptic clung to her lab coat, a reminder of the sterile world she inhabited beyond these walls.

"Mr. Voss," she said, her voice barely above a whisper. "I apologize for the intrusion, but there's been a development."

Voss raised an eyebrow, inviting her to continue. The air between them crackled with unspoken tension.

"The latest batch of stem cells," Dr. Chen continued, her fingers fidgeting with the tablet she carried. "They're… reacting in ways we've never seen before. The cellular regeneration rates are off the charts, but—"

She hesitated, and Voss felt a chill of anticipation run down his spine.

"But?" he prompted, his voice low and controlled.

Dr. Chen's eyes turned to the ornate box on the table behind him, a flicker of suspicion crossing her features. "The genetic markers are unstable. We're seeing rapid mutations, almost as if the cells are trying to rewrite their own DNA. It's unlike anything in our previous trials."

Voss's mind raced, connecting the dots between the bone fragments and this new development. Could it be that the essence he sought was already manifesting, even before full integration?

"Show me," he commanded, gesturing toward the door.

As they left the museum, the weight of possibility pressed down on Voss's shoulders. He cast one last glance at the box containing Peter's bones, a small smile playing at the corners of his mouth. The path to immortality was never meant to be smooth, but he was prepared to face whatever challenges lay ahead.

The corridor stretched before them, leading toward the labs where the future of humanity was being rewritten, one cell at a time. With each step, Voss felt the thrill of discovery mingling with the intoxicating allure of power. Whatever awaited in those petri dishes, he was certain of one thing—there was no turning back now.

CHAPTER
THIRTY-SEVEN

Voss followed Dr. Chen through the long, dim corridor that connected his private museum to the estate's cutting-edge laboratory wing. The walls were lined with abstract sculptures, each piece meant to inspire boldness and innovation, but Voss's attention was elsewhere, his mind racing. If the cells had indeed begun mutating as Dr. Chen described, his plans might be moving forward faster than he had anticipated.

They entered the lab, the air cold and sterile, the faint hum of machinery adding an almost ominous undercurrent. Dr. Chen walked briskly to a workstation where her laptop connected to a series of monitors, each screen alive with microscopic images, genetic code sequences, and cellular diagrams. She tapped a few keys, and the image of a petri dish appeared, magnified, showing a cluster of cells moving with an energy that felt almost... conscious.

"These are the stem cells we cultivated from the latest batch," Dr. Chen explained, her voice focused and methodical. "At first, they behaved normally. But then, around hour six, the regenerative rates spiked to levels we've only theorized about, and the cellular structures began shifting. It's as though they're adapting—rewriting themselves."

She tapped the screen, and the image zoomed in further, displaying close-up shots of the cells. Voss studied them with rapt attention. Each cell seemed to pulse, dividing and regenerating at a rate that defied even the boldest projections of their research. But the mutations Dr. Chen mentioned were visible as well—tiny distortions in the DNA strands, flickers of instability amid the otherwise miraculous replication.

"Have you isolated the genetic anomalies?" Voss asked, his voice steady as he leaned closer, studying the screen.

Dr. Chen nodded. "Yes. I've been tracking the mutation sites." She pulled up another image, a strand of DNA with specific segments highlighted in red. "These sequences here—they're unlike anything in the human genome. They're almost… foreign, as if something is trying to merge with the cells' natural composition."

Voss felt a surge of excitement. The nature of these anomalies only confirmed his suspicions that the source of power he sought wasn't just theoretical. The bones contained something real—something that could change everything. He watched the screen, his eyes gleaming with ambition.

"This instability," he asked, keeping his tone casual, "is it dangerous?"

Dr. Chen hesitated, her fingers hovering over the keyboard. "That's the problem, Mr. Voss. If we continue the trials without addressing these mutations, we could be looking at rapid cellular breakdowns—or worse. But if we could stabilize the changes..."

She trailed off, her voice filled with the thrill of scientific discovery but with the edge of uncertainty. Voss knew that Dr. Chen had no knowledge of the bones. She believed this was merely another experiment in cellular regeneration, an attempt to push human limits. But he could see the subtle signs of her suspicion, her careful glances at the ornate box he had left in the museum, her curious silence about the origins of this project.

"Stabilization will come," he assured her smoothly, "but first, we need to observe. Give the cells a chance to fully adapt."

She glanced at him, her brows furrowing in concern, but she nodded. "I'll leave them for observation overnight. There are live feeds set up to monitor the cellular activity in real time."

He nodded, pleased with her efficiency. "Excellent." Voss inclined his head. "Thank you, Dr. Chen. I'll monitor things here."

A beat of silence passed as Dr. Chen studied him, and for a moment, he saw the curiosity flicker in her eyes again, the questions she was holding back. But then she turned, the professional mask slipping back into place.

"I'll be in the east wing, running analysis on the genetic sequencing. Call if there are any changes," she said, her voice steady but with an edge of reserve.

She left the lab, the quiet hiss of the door sliding shut marking her exit. The moment she was gone, Voss's expression changed, the composed mask giving way to something darker, more intense. Alone, he approached the petri dish under the microscope, his gaze intent. He watched as the cells continued to pulse and mutate, the rapid divisions reflecting the frantic energy of life struggling against limitation.

He reached for a small vial filled with a minuscule sample of a serum he had been perfecting—a serum designed to amplify the regenerative properties of ancient DNA. Carefully, he added a single drop into the petri dish, watching with fascination as the cells absorbed the liquid. The pulsing intensified, the cells glowing faintly as the serum took effect, and Voss's heart raced as he saw the mutations stabilize, the structure becoming more robust, as if accepting this new form.

"Perfect," he whispered, his voice filled with awe and a hint of reverence.

He knew that what he was doing crossed every ethical boundary. He had bypassed the standard protocols, concealed the origins of the research from Dr. Chen, and lied to his entire team. But none of that mattered. The path to immortality wasn't one to be tread lightly. It required risk, secrecy, and an unwavering vision.

In that moment, watching the cells dance under the

microscope, Voss saw a glimmer of his dream realized—the possibility of a human body that could regenerate, adapt, evolve beyond the ordinary limitations of time. His mind spun with visions of what he would become, what he would create—a new genesis, built upon the very foundation of humanity's origins, one in which he would play the role of creator and ultimate benefactor.

Tomorrow, the work would continue, with Dr. Chen none the wiser. For now, he allowed himself to revel in the first tangible proof of his theory, the bones' latent power merging with science to create something extraordinary.

He leaned back, watching the cells continue their rapid, stable growth, a dark satisfaction settling over him.

THIRTY-EIGHT

Michael closed the heavy oak door to Matteo Ferrante's office in the Apostolic Palace, feeling the familiar weight of the marble walls pressing in around him. The room was quiet, lit by a single brass lamp on the corner of Matteo's desk. Matteo looked up, his face a blend of concern and curiosity, sensing that Michael's visit wasn't a casual one.

"Michael," he greeted the priest, motioning to the chair opposite him. "It's late. What brings you here at this hour?"

Michael sat, his fingers interlaced, and exhaled deeply. He had thought carefully about what to say, but now, sitting before Matteo, the reality of his confession felt heavier than he had anticipated.

"Matteo," he began quietly, "I need to share something with you—something I've kept to myself until now." He paused, gathering his thoughts. "You're aware, of course, that this exhibition of the relics was a high-risk endeavor from the beginning. St. Peter's bones... they're among the Church's most sacred treasures."

Matteo nodded slowly, his gaze sharpening. "Yes, and we did all we could to ensure their security. But... something tells me there's more?"

Michael nodded, leaning forward. "There's much more. I have reason to believe that someone—someone with considerable influence—planned to swap St. Peter's bones with counterfeits, replicas indistinguishable from the originals to the untrained eye."

Matteo's eyes widened, his brow furrowing with alarm. "Swapped? But that would mean..."

"That they intended to steal the relics for themselves," Michael finished. "And my suspicions pointed directly to Elliot Voss. He was heavily involved in supporting the exhibition, offering resources and connections, but all the while, I sensed his interests extended beyond mere philanthropy."

Matteo's expression darkened, and he sat back, absorbing the revelation. "And you believe Voss went through with it?"

"Yes. During the blackout yesterday," Michael replied. "It was brief, but it was enough. I've already reviewed the security footage. I watched him stand by as the lights flickered, his movements calculated. He orchestrated the switch in those few seconds."

Matteo's jaw clenched, his voice tense. "Then... the

bones on display now, the ones venerated by thousands of pilgrims—*they're fakes?!*"

"Replicas, yes," Michael confirmed, his voice steady. "But Voss's replicas."

Matteo frowned, looking at Michael with dawning realization. "But… what do you mean…?"

Michael nodded. "I suspected Voss might make a move, so I took my own precaution. The day before the exhibition began, I removed the authentic bones of St. Peter and replaced them with the comparable remains of a lesser-known early Christian from our archives. Voss walked away with nothing more than someone else's bones—but certainly not Peter's."

Matteo exhaled, his shoulders relaxing just slightly as the revelation settled over him. But there was still concern in his eyes. "Michael, what about the pilgrims? Thousands have come here to venerate these relics, and we've allowed them to venerate… imitations?"

A shadow of doubt crossed Michael's face, and he looked down for a moment before meeting Matteo's gaze. "It hasn't been easy, Matteo. I've struggled with it more than you know. I've watched the faithful pour in, hoping to touch the divine, seeking connection with our faith's very foundations. And yet, they kneel before… another's bones." He sighed, running a hand down his face. "I've wrestled with this more than I can say. But in the end, I've come to see that their prayers—their veneration—are directed not at the bones themselves but at the legacy they represent. A legacy I'm charged to protect, and I feared this was the only way to safeguard the real relics."

Matteo's eyes softened, though he remained silent, letting Michael continue.

"It's a difficult truth to accept, but I believe that faith is what sanctifies the relics, Matteo. Not the relics themselves." Michael's voice grew stronger, more resolute. "The prayers of the faithful aren't diminished by what lies within that glass case. The people come here to touch the legacy of Peter, the apostle who laid the foundation for the Church, who died for his faith, who became the rock upon which we build our lives. That devotion—that belief—is what gives these relics their sanctity."

Matteo was quiet for a long moment, his gaze shifting to the small crucifix on his desk as he weighed Michael's words. He nodded slowly, understanding dawning in his expression. "I see your point, Michael. Their prayers, their faith, are rooted in the symbol, not the substance."

"Precisely," Michael said, relief flooding his voice. "For those who believe, this is a moment of spiritual connection, and I couldn't bear the thought of risking St. Peter's actual remains, especially knowing that someone like Voss might walk away with them. The bones are safe in the vault, untouched, where they'll remain for as long as necessary."

Matteo's expression softened, a faint smile pulling at the corner of his mouth. "You always have been more perceptive than most, Michael. I can't imagine many would have anticipated such a move by Voss."

Michael smiled, though his expression remained thoughtful. "I only hope that, in the end, I've done right by both the Church and the faithful. Deception of any kind leaves a mark. But if it keeps the legacy of Peter secure, then... I believe it's a mark I can live with."

Matteo nodded, his respect for Michael evident in his steady gaze. "You've protected not only the Church's most sacred relics but also the spirit of devotion that surrounds them. That's no small feat."

"Thank you, Matteo." Michael's voice subsided, a hint of relief in his tone. "I'll continue watching Voss, ensuring that his interference ends here. The bones of St. Peter will remain where they belong, safe and undisturbed."

Matteo placed a reassuring hand on Michael's shoulder. "And as always, Michael, you have my full support."

They sat together in quiet understanding, two guardians of faith and history, bound by a shared mission to protect the legacy of the Church, even in the face of modern threats.

THIRTY-NINE

Michael sat in his office, the late afternoon sun casting long shadows across the worn wooden desk. He tapped his fingers lightly against the phone, his mind racing as he prepared his approach. Accusing Voss directly would get him nowhere—the man was far too slippery. But Michael had a plan, a carefully constructed line of questioning that might just unnerve Voss enough to reveal something useful. He took a slow breath, calming himself, then dialed Voss's number.

The phone rang twice before Voss picked up, his smooth, familiar voice on the other end. "Father Dominic," he greeted, a note of amusement in his tone. "To what do I owe the pleasure?"

Michael forced a casual tone. "Elliot. I know you've probably just touched down back in Seattle, but I wanted to check in about the exhibition. There were…

well, some unexpected developments with the reliquary."

There was a pause, brief but telling. "Oh? I wasn't aware of anything unusual when I left. What sort of developments?"

Michael leaned back in his chair, carefully crafting his words. "We had a bit of a situation earlier today— small but unusual. It seems someone may have... tampered with the bones on display. Switched them with fakes, to be more precise."

He let the words hang, listening to the silence stretch across the line.

"That's... surprising," Voss replied, his tone mild, though Michael could sense the undertone of tension. "I'd imagine security was tighter than that. Are you certain?"

"Quite," Michael said, keeping his voice steady. "In fact, the swap was fairly sophisticated. They weren't just random replicas, Elliot. Someone went to great lengths to ensure they looked the part." He allowed a pause, hoping the implication would settle in. "But thankfully, I'd taken certain precautions, given the high-profile nature of the exhibition. The real loss, you see, was rather minimal."

"Precautions?" Voss repeated, his tone laced with a desperate curiosity. "And what exactly do you mean by that?"

Michael allowed himself a small smile, keeping his tone light. "Let's just say that St. Peter's bones hold a unique place in the Church. I wasn't about to risk exposing them to the public. The exhibition was mostly symbolic—a gesture, if you will. So, yes, I took precautions."

A longer silence followed, and Michael imagined Voss's mind whirring, trying to piece together the implications. Michael hoped the hint would unsettle him, forcing him to rethink his own confidence in what he had taken.

"It's good to hear you were so careful, Father Dominic," Voss finally said, his voice even, though Michael detected a slight edge. "I suppose it's fortunate then that whoever tried to interfere with the display will come up empty-handed."

"Yes," Michael replied smoothly. "Though it's troubling to think someone would go to such lengths. It makes one wonder who would be interested in taking such risks."

"Indeed," Voss murmured. "But you don't have any suspects yet, I assume?"

"Oh, none confirmed," Michael said lightly, "but these things have a way of revealing themselves over time. Especially when certain parties realize what they've gained... or perhaps lost."

The faint sound of a breath on the other end of the line hinted at Voss's attempt to maintain composure. "I'm sure you'll get to the bottom of it, Michael. After all, you've always had a talent for uncovering secrets."

Michael smiled, sensing the conversation was steering exactly where he wanted. "I try my best. And Elliot... I'll be reaching out again soon. You know, just to keep you in the loop as this unfolds. I wouldn't want you missing out on any developments."

"Of course," Voss replied, a trace of forced casualness slipping into his tone. "I'd be glad to hear how it all turns out. Take care, Father Dominic."

"And you, Elliot," Michael said, a final hint of satisfaction lacing his words as he ended the call.

He set the phone down, a faint smile crossing his lips. If he had planted even the smallest seed of doubt in Voss's mind, it would be worth it. The game had just begun, and Michael knew that soon enough, Voss would start questioning what he thought he had won for his fifty million dollars.

CHAPTER
FORTY

V oss set the phone down, his hand clenched tightly around it, his knuckles white against the polished surface of his desk. Michael's words echoed in his mind, gnawing at his certainty.

The real loss was minimal. He'd taken precautions. The bones on display were mostly symbolic. Voss felt his pulse quicken, a surge of anger rising within him as doubt began to creep into his mind.

Could it be possible? Had Michael switched the bones before Voss's own careful swap? He looked over at the ornate box, still resting on the seat beside him, containing what he believed were St. Peter's bones. He had carried it back to Seattle with the assurance that he now possessed a relic of unparalleled power and significance. But Michael's hints, his cool, measured tone—there was no mistaking the calculated nature of the priest's words. Michael had wanted him to second-guess, to question the very thing Voss had worked so meticulously to obtain.

Furious, Voss stood and paced across his private study, his mind racing as he replayed every detail of the Vatican operation. He had executed his plan flawlessly, created a distraction, orchestrated the blackout, and moved swiftly to exchange the bones in the reliquary. Every step had gone according to plan. And yet… Michael's words. Had he underestimated the priest? Had Michael somehow anticipated the move, replaced the true bones with something else before Voss even had a chance to get his hands on them? Or was he playing a game, knowing there was a swap and pretending that Voss didn't have the real ones?

He took a deep breath, fighting the impulse to pick up the box and smash it against the wall. For all his calculated planning, all his supposed foresight, he was beginning to feel like he was standing on shifting sands. *No*, he told himself, *the bones were authentic*. His contacts, his access to Vatican reports, the replicas he himself had crafted based on the precise measurements he had obtained—all pointed to the authenticity of what he now held. But could it be that Michael had staged the entire setup to make him believe he had succeeded? The thought made his stomach churn.

Voss's jaw clenched. He wouldn't allow himself to be outmaneuvered. If Michael had somehow anticipated him, if he had prepared for this, then Voss would find out. And he would have his revenge.

He moved toward the box, lifting it with a renewed determination, his fingers gripping the edges tightly. He needed to know if he had been deceived, and there were ways to find out. The bones would undergo further testing. He would summon his scientists, the best geneticists he had in his pocket, and they would analyze every molecule, every trace of DNA. If the bones were a fake, they would know.

But Michael's voice, cool and calm, lingered in his mind. *"I'd taken certain precautions... the real loss was rather minimal."*

Was it all a trap? Voss felt his heart race, fury bubbling beneath his controlled exterior. If Michael had toyed with him, if this entire effort had been for nothing, he wouldn't take it lightly. He would confront the priest, force him to reveal what he knew. The Vatican's secrets weren't as tightly held as they thought. Voss had ways of prying information from even the most well-guarded institutions, and Michael was no exception.

Voss's fingers trembled slightly as he unlatched the ornate box, the soft click echoing in the stillness of his study. The air felt thick, charged with tension as he slowly lifted the lid. The bones inside lay nestled on a bed of deep crimson velvet, their ivory surface dull in the muted light. He reached in, hesitating for a moment before grasping one of the smaller fragments.

The bone felt cool against his skin, its weight both substantial and unnervingly light. Voss turned it over in his palm, scrutinizing every curve and crevice. To his untrained eye, it appeared genuine—ancient, brittle, with the patina of centuries. But doubt gnawed at him, Michael's words a persistent whisper in his mind. A knock at the door startled him. Voss quickly replaced the bone and snapped the box shut, his heart pounding.

"Enter," he called, forcing his voice to remain steady.

His assistant, Julia, stepped inside. Her dark eyes swept over him, concern etched on her face. "Sir, the lab team is ready. They're waiting for your instructions."

Voss nodded curtly, gathering himself. "Tell them to prepare for a full spectral analysis. I want DNA sequencing, carbon dating, the works."

Julia hesitated, her gaze flickering to the box. "And the… item in question?"

"I'll bring it down myself," Voss replied, his tone brooking no further discussion.

As Julia left, Voss turned back to the window, Seattle's skyline a glittering tapestry beyond the glass. Night had fallen, the city's lights coming alive like a constellation of earthbound stars. But the beauty was lost on him, his mind consumed by the game he now realized he was playing—a game where the stakes were higher than he had ever imagined.

He picked up the box, its weight suddenly oppressive. As he moved towards the door, a chill ran down his spine. He couldn't shake the feeling that somewhere, in some shadowy corner the Vatican, Michael was smiling, already several moves ahead in a chess match Voss hadn't even known he was playing.

The elevator ride down to the lab felt interminable. Voss's reflection stared back at him from the polished doors—a man on edge, his usual confidence replaced by a haunted look in his eyes. The box seemed to pulse in his hands, a Pandora's vessel of secrets and lies.

As the doors slid open, revealing the sterile white corridor of his private research facility, Voss steeled himself. Whatever the truth, whatever game Michael was playing, he would unravel it. And when he did, there would be a reckoning. The bones of St. Peter—real or fake—were just the beginning. The true prize lay in the power they represented, and Voss was determined to claim it, no matter the cost.

FORTY-ONE

T wo days later, Voss sat alone in his office, the lights dimmed. His fingers drummed impatiently against the armrest of his chair as he stared at the closed envelope in front of him. Inside were the results of the analysis—a full battery of tests he had ordered, from carbon dating to DNA sequencing, all aimed at confirming what should have been a certainty: that the bones in question were those of St. Peter.

Michael Dominic's probing questions had rattled him, raising doubts that he had been unwilling to consider. But now, with these test results, he would finally have the clarity he needed. He reached for the envelope and took a steadying breath before tearing it open.

As he read through the initial report, a wave of relief washed over him. The carbon dating had come back with an astonishingly precise range: first century, perfectly aligning with the period of Peter's life. Voss felt a small, triumphant smile tugging at the corners of his mouth. *First century*—exactly the timeframe he had needed. If the bones were that old, it was one step closer to certainty.

But as he read further, his satisfaction began to erode. There was a notation about geographic origin. DNA analysis couldn't definitively place someone's birthplace, but mitochondrial DNA could suggest regional affiliations, indicating where a person's maternal ancestors might have lived.

A frown deepened on Voss's face as he saw the words:

Maternal haplogroup: consistent with regions slightly east of traditional Judea.

HE FELT the blood drain from his face. *Eastern Judea?* Peter had been a Galilean fisherman, a man from the region surrounding the Sea of Galilee. If these were his bones, wouldn't the DNA results match that origin? The implication was subtle but unmistakable: the bones could belong to someone from a different region altogether, likely from among the early Christian communities but not definitively tied to Peter's homeland.

Voss's mind raced as he tried to reconcile this anomaly. The timeframe fit, but the regional markers didn't. Still, it wasn't enough to disprove the bones' authenticity outright. Galilee wasn't far from eastern Judea—it was plausible, at least in theory, that someone in Peter's family line could have come from another region. But the doubts gnawed at him, like shadows flickering in the corner of his mind.

He pushed the report aside and picked up the analysis summary from the osteological examination. The wear and injury patterns were consistent with what could be expected of a man who had led a hard life, possibly marked by travel and hardship. One of the bones bore evidence of old breaks—healed fractures, suggestive of a person who had endured physical trauma. This could fit Peter, who had faced multiple imprisonments and hardships during his mission.

But then his eyes caught another notation:

Presence of mineral deposits consistent with exposure to regions outside of Italy.

Voss clenched his jaw. The implication was maddening. The mineral traces suggested the bones might have come from an environment foreign to Rome—specifically, a soil composition that indicated exposure to areas north of Rome, possibly Gaul or Germania, but not definitively so. The faintest trace of an unusual pollen was also found on the bones, a type that hadn't been identified in the immediate Roman vicinity. It was another layer of mystery, another sliver of evidence that led him away from any definitive answer.

Voss leaned back in his chair, frustration bubbling beneath his calm exterior. He had assumed the bones had always been kept in Rome since they had supposedly been laid to rest in the Vatican's care. But if these findings were accurate, then they might have traveled before reaching Rome. He felt the thrill of revelation tempered by the gnawing fear of what this could mean. *Was it possible that the bones had been moved or even replaced centuries ago?*

And then there was one final result—one last line of the report that his eyes locked onto, the line that nearly made him laugh in disbelief:

Anomalous DNA sequence found in one of the samples; not consistent with typical Mediterranean markers, potentially a rare haplogroup associated with populations found farther east of traditional Judea.

THIS WAS IT. Voss's mind reeled as he processed this detail. The bones were close to a match but not exact, as if they were a decoy, planted by someone with enough knowledge to make it convincing but not foolproof. This possibility, however outrageous, made a terrible sort of sense. *What if the bones he possessed were a substitution, a switch from antiquity, meant to protect the real relics by leaving a stand-in?*

Voss's carefully laid confidence cracked. He had thought he held Peter's remains. He had considered the risks and rewards of the exhibition, convinced of its significance, of the Vatican's own certainty about the authenticity of the bones. But now, these findings left him questioning everything. He had seen enough in his line of work to know that ancient deceptions were far from uncommon. *Could early Christians have created a decoy, using another martyr's bones to divert attention from Peter's true remains?*

Voss felt a chill spread through him. If that were true, the implications were immense. The Church had venerated these bones for centuries, and now, as he sat staring at the results, he realized that the truth might never be fully known. Even as he wanted to brush it aside, to assume these bones were Peter's, he knew his team's findings would haunt him.

The most logical step would be to keep the doubts hidden. After all, the bones had already been authenticated multiple times over the centuries; the carbon dating matched; the injuries and hardships suggested a man of Peter's life story. Voss considered the power of appearances. Perhaps it was best to let the faithful believe. After all, *certainty* was the foundation of belief, even if it was built on careful ambiguity.

But Michael Dominic… That thought jolted him. Dominic's questions, his relentless pursuit of the truth, had already unsettled Voss, and he knew the priest wouldn't stop now.

The envelope lay open on his desk, its contents a potent mix of truth and illusion, facts that danced on the edge of certainty but fell just short. With a surge of irritation, Voss closed the report, his mind whirling with conflicting thoughts. He had options, but none were perfect. He could bury the report, push forward with his plans, and not question the bones' authenticity. Or he could alter his plans, orchestrate a way to cover his theft if Michael ever produced evidence of it.

One thing was certain: he could no longer proceed with the confidence he'd had before. Michael Dominic was already suspicious. And if he continued to probe, continued to dig deeper, he would eventually discover that the bones being presented as St. Peter's were fakes. Whether the ones Voss had stolen were Peter's wouldn't matter; only the fact that Voss had switched fakes with the bones that had been on display.

Voss sat back in his chair, feeling the weight of the decision he had to make pressing down on him. He would move forward, but he would do so carefully, aware of the thin line he walked.

But one thing he couldn't shake—the feeling that he was now part of a deception much older than himself. Whether he liked it or not, he was now a player in a game of shadows, one that potentially stretched back to the earliest days of the Church. And if Michael kept prying, Voss knew that sooner or later, the full truth—whatever it was—would come to light.

FORTY-TWO

In the soft light of his office, Father Michael Dominic leaned back, fingers steepled, as he considered the last words he had exchanged with Elliot Voss over the phone. Voss's voice had held a certain tremor, his confidence slipping, undercut by Michael's pointed questions about authenticity. And there lay the seed of doubt, as Michael had intended. But how much leverage could he truly gain from pursuing Voss any further?

He drew in a deep breath and let it out slowly, his gaze drifting toward the narrow window that framed the centuries-old buildings of Vatican City. What was it he sought to accomplish by pushing harder? Even if he did, what might he truly uncover?

Michael thought of the nine authentic bone fragments now resting in the reliquary, proudly displayed beneath bulletproof glass. The bones were revered, cloaked in sanctity, and watched over by Swiss

Guards with unrelenting vigilance. Their authenticity, at least as declared by the Church, had been established long ago. But authenticity, as Voss likely now understood, was as much about faith and reverence as it was about evidence.

Michael felt the corners of his lips turn upward, almost involuntarily. Voss was swimming in circles of his own creation, grappling with authenticity as he fumbled in the dark. By drawing Voss into this dance of suspicion, Michael had handed him nothing concrete— just enough bait to leave him questioning the value of the very prize he sought to replicate.

What would come of pressing Voss to confess? Michael considered this angle carefully. The Vatican was a fortress of secrets, some whispers of which had lingered for centuries, evolving into myths and legends. Voss's ambitions, though perilous, were hardly the gravest threat the Church had ever faced. To expose Voss's deceit—if he could even do so with certainty— might offer some justice. But what would it accomplish, truly? Voss would only work harder to shield his activities, deepening his reach into the archives with covert attempts to outmaneuver Michael's every move.

And besides, the very existence of an imposter set of relics had little bearing on the true bones resting securely behind Vatican walls. Voss was chasing after a shadow—a grand illusion of power that would elude him, even if he succeeded in fabricating the entire display.

Leaning forward, Michael drummed his fingers on the oak desk, a final thought crystallizing in his mind.

Voss's frantic call for legitimacy, his desperate moves to replicate relics he could barely comprehend, would be his own undoing. Letting Voss thrash in the murky waters of his own doubts was, perhaps, the only course that preserved both the sanctity of the relics and the dignity of the Church.

Why chase him down a dark, uncertain path when he was already stumbling toward the edge on his own?

With a sigh, Michael stood up, the decision settling within him. He would leave the matter be. His words, strategic yet ambiguous, had already sown the seeds of doubt. Now, Voss would be left to wrestle with his own ambitions, and Michael would be free to focus on the greater mysteries within the archives, the secrets that were worth more than the truth of a single relic.

With a final glance out the window, he murmured to himself, "Let the man drown in his own uncertainty." And with that, he closed the file on Voss, ready to move forward into the deeper shadows of his work.

CHAPTER

FORTY-THREE

As evening shadows lengthened across the walls of the Vatican, Michael sat in his office, a sense of quiet expectancy filling the room. He had set aside the intrigue surrounding Elliot Voss, relegating it to a closed chapter, at least for now. His attention was now consumed by the weightier matter of the Peter-Linus inscriptions—a mystery imbued with the origins of the Church and the line of succession that could reshape the historical understanding of early Christian leadership.

A firm knock sounded on the door, and in strode Marcus Russo, the archaeologist Michael had relied upon for years. Marcus carried an old leather folio, worn from use, filled with notes and transcripts. Michael gestured for him to sit, and Marcus took the chair across from him, placing the folio on the desk between them.

"Good evening, Father Michael," Marcus began,

nodding with a slight smile. "I brought as much as I could fit in this"—he tapped the folio—"without overwhelming us. The team's research on the Peter-Linus inscriptions has been... well, revelatory."

Michael leaned forward, his curiosity keen. "Then let's dive in. What do we know so far about Linus's role in those early years?"

Marcus drew a deep breath, organizing his thoughts. "Well, Linus remains one of the most enigmatic figures in the Church's history, largely because he lived in Peter's shadow. But the inscriptions we found near the Catacombs of St. Callixtus suggest a far more substantial role than previously assumed. Some of the inscriptions carry phrases that translate to 'the one who guards the keys' or even, 'the one who guides in Peter's name.' This points to a period when Linus may have acted with near papal authority."

Michael's eyes narrowed. "You're suggesting he was more than a mere placeholder? That he was trusted by Peter not just as a caretaker but as someone who actively shaped the community?"

"Exactly." Marcus opened the folio and pulled out a few photographs of the inscriptions, each marked with annotations in Latin and Greek. "Several historians I brought in have corroborated this theory. One of the phrases, inscribed almost as if it were a title, reads 'Pontifex Linus Custodis Fidei'—'Linus, Guardian of the Faith.' The title is similar to one typically associated with Peter. This suggests a formalized authority, potentially signaling that Peter saw Linus as his successor in matters of faith and doctrine. And that was the way it had always been interpreted before this—that Linus was Peter's intended successor."

Michael studied the photos intently, his fingers tracing the faint lines of Latin etched in stone. "This inscription... it could also be taken another way, especially if written while Peter was alive. It complicates the early succession narrative. We've always assumed that Peter's role as the rock upon which the Church was built would transfer in a clear line. Yet if Linus was 'the Guardian of the Faith,' as Peter was, it implies a parallel line of authority."

Marcus nodded. "It's possible that, during Peter's later years but before his death, Linus was given more than just administrative duties. Early documents don't specify much about Linus's actual functions, but these inscriptions paint a picture of someone actively shaping theological thought, even mediating disputes."

"That would place him not as a secondary figure but as a primary leader," Michael mused. "What about the timing? Does it fit with the persecutions under Nero?"

"Precisely." Marcus's voice took on an air of reverence, as if he could feel the solemnity of the ages pressing upon them. "In fact, some of the inscriptions explicitly reference persecution. There are phrases alluding to Nero as 'the beast' and to Linus 'leading the faithful underground.' We know Nero's persecution of the Christians occurred in AD 64, as he used them as the scapegoat for his own burning of Rome. And St. Peter was crucified sometime between 64 and 68 AD. So if these inscriptions are accurate, then Linus wasn't just managing an institution; he was the face of the Church to the community, rallying people, preserving teachings, even performing rites while Peter was still alive as well."

Michael leaned back, absorbing this revelation. "If Linus was acting as the 'Guardian of the Faith' during those dark years, he would have shaped the Church's doctrines under siege. His role wouldn't have been administrative alone; he would've been forced to make decisions about what survived and what didn't— decisions that could've influenced theology profoundly."

"Exactly. Our team suspects that Linus, rather than simply holding Peter's place after his death, may have functioned as a kind of bishop or even proto-pope, preserving teachings and leading when Peter was imprisoned or in hiding. It's like he was Peter's shadow, a silent partner keeping the Church alive from the background."

Michael stared at Marcus, a deep realization dawning. "So, Linus may have determined which teachings to preserve, what to emphasize... That would mean much of what we attribute to Peter as doctrine could have Linus's fingerprints on it."

Marcus nodded thoughtfully, taking a small packet of loose-leaf notes from the folio. "And that's just it. Our historians discovered something fascinating among the later documents we found—letters and fragments of early Christian writing that mention teachings or parables 'as instructed by Linus.' If this is authentic, then Linus wasn't merely following Peter or his successor."

Michael's voice softened, almost in reverence. "So this isn't merely the story of Peter passing a torch. Linus could have adapted the Church's teachings to protect it, to make it resilient."

"Exactly," Marcus said with a glint of excitement in his eyes. "And it's this adaptability that could have allowed the Church to survive the brutal early years of persecution. Linus may have forged that resilience, unwittingly preparing the Church for the trials it would endure under Roman scrutiny."

The two sat in silence for a moment, absorbing the profound implications of Marcus's research. Michael could feel a thrill building within him, the gravity of what they had uncovered settling around them like a mantle.

Marcus broke the silence first. "If Linus was indeed responsible for shaping the Church's early resilience, then his influence goes far beyond the administrative. He would've been setting precedents, deciding how to guide and comfort the faithful, even developing early doctrine under Peter's name but, ultimately, under his own guidance."

"This complicates our understanding of early Church history," Michael said quietly. "If Linus was as integral to the faith as Peter, then the line of succession isn't simply Peter to Linus to Clement. It's... intertwined."

"Perhaps that's what Peter wanted," Marcus said softly. "If Peter was entrusting Linus with his legacy, it may have been because he saw in Linus the same drive to protect and shape the faith, a kindred spirit. Not as a replacement, but as a continuation—a safeguard, a way for the faith to survive regardless of who wore the mantle of authority."

Michael nodded, a sense of clarity settling over him. "It's almost as if Linus's role was to protect the Church from within, a guardian of its earliest doctrines, while Peter, as the public rock, faced Rome and all its dangers."

"Exactly," Marcus replied. "It's a dual role—one who faced the world, and one who guarded the Church from within."

They sat in silence again, their thoughts trailing down the corridors of history, of hidden influence and veiled power. Linus's legacy, obscured for centuries, was emerging not as a mere footnote in Peter's shadow, but as a quiet force that had shaped the Church's resilience and its doctrine.

Michael finally spoke, his voice a murmur. "We'll need to study this further. This knowledge… it's a missing piece of our origins, a glimpse into the Church's foundations. It's not just history, Marcus—it's a revelation."

Marcus's eyes gleamed with excitement. "The team and I are at your disposal, Father Michael. There's more here, hidden in inscriptions and fragments, and we're only just beginning."

The two men sat in contemplative silence, the weight of the centuries between Linus's hidden chamber and the present moment binding them to a legacy they now carried forward. In this quiet understanding, Michael felt renewed purpose—a charge, perhaps, to ensure that the faith Linus so valiantly protected remained steadfast, preserved for all those yet to come.

As Marcus gathered his papers and prepared to leave, Michael placed a hand on the folio, holding it in place for just a moment. "This discovery," he said softly, "is why we do what we do. Thank you, Marcus. Let's bring Linus into the light."

And as Marcus departed, leaving the folio and his notes for further study, Michael felt the burden of legacy shift. The past, it seemed, wasn't a silent guardian; it spoke, quietly and insistently, waiting for someone to listen. And in that listening, the truths of their faith would be revealed anew.

FORTY-FOUR

I n the shadows of his sprawling Hunt's Point estate, Elliot Voss sat by the floor-to-ceiling window that overlooked the rain-slicked Seattle cityscape, the skyline shrouded in mist beneath the ever-present gray. The world outside felt distant, like some faded painting hanging on the wall—utterly meaningless, a mere backdrop to his frustration and disbelief.

The fire that had once fueled him to chase after St. Peter's bones now felt like embers dying in a rainstorm. For months, he had poured his resources, his network, and even his soul into one single, all-consuming ambition: to forge a link with St. Peter, the rock upon which the Church itself was built. He had believed that securing Peter's DNA, blending it with his own in some alchemical ritual of science and spirituality, would open a doorway to eternity. But here he was, grasping at nothing but ashes.

Voss glanced at his reflection in the dark glass, his face half-shadowed, hollow-eyed. The past weeks played over in his mind—a series of steps so calculated, yet all leading to ruin. Father Michael Dominic, with his quiet presence and unsettlingly calm demeanor, had dismantled his plans with nothing more than a few well-placed questions, an understated skepticism that had left Voss second-guessing every detail. There was something insidious about the way the priest had handled him. Nothing overt, nothing tangible—just enough to sow doubt, to poison the clarity of his once-rigid ambitions.

"Did he know?" Voss muttered aloud, his voice barely above a whisper, as though he feared the priest's presence might still linger, hovering in the recesses of his mind. "Did he know what I was trying to do all along?" The thought chilled him and he shook his head, forcing himself back into control. He couldn't bear to admit that he, Elliot Voss, had been outplayed. But the seed had been planted, and with it came the inevitable question: had he been a fool?

As he replayed his plans, Voss couldn't ignore the grim absurdity of what he had once believed to be a brilliant scheme. He had ventured into uncharted territory, crossing lines no other man would even dare to approach, all for the chance to hold within himself the remnants of Peter's legacy. But for what? To attain immortality? Or had it been about something else— some desperate need to transcend his own limitations, to build his own mythology from the bones of another?

The more he thought about it, the more he realized

how grotesque his ambitions truly were. He had envisioned it all so clearly: a laboratory illuminated by sterile fluorescent light, scientists standing by as he underwent an injection of genetically reconstructed material. He had imagined feeling a surge, some mystical connection to a man long dead, a conduit to eternity. But now, the fantasy felt morbid, obscene even. The thought of injecting his own body with the genetic markers of a saint repulsed him, and a cold shiver ran down his spine as he confronted the lunacy of it all.

"What was I thinking?" he murmured to himself, running a hand over his face. He couldn't deny it anymore—the pursuit had changed him, twisted him, led him down paths of delusion. He had convinced himself that the essence of sainthood, of legacy, of immortality itself, could be extracted like some rare mineral and grafted onto his own life. How had he fallen so far?

There was a bitterness in his stomach, a creeping awareness that what he had sought all along wasn't greatness, but simply an escape from his own mortality. A desperate attempt to leave behind something more than money, more than power. He had wanted to defy the inevitable, to rewrite his own story with the bones of an apostle, but it had been nothing more than hubris. And now, in the cold light of his own mind, he saw that for what it was—a fantasy, one doomed to fail from the start.

The memory of Father Dominic's final words, laced with subtle implications, returned to him, and Voss felt a flare of anger ignite within him. That priest, so unassuming yet cunning, had seen through his façade, picked apart his ambitions as if they were mere strands of fiction. Michael Dominic hadn't thwarted him directly, hadn't confronted him with accusations or challenges. Instead, he had done something far worse— he had left Voss to confront himself, to realize the emptiness of his plans on his own.

Elliot Voss gritted his teeth, his hands clenching as he stood, pacing the length of the room. The anger surged and faded, replaced by a dark acceptance. He would never get what he wanted; the dream was shattered. Michael Dominic was likely sitting in his office in Rome, smug in his victory, content to leave Voss to stew in his defeat. And what stung most of all was that Dominic hadn't needed to lift a finger to see him fail. It had been his own ambitions, his own blindness, that had led him to ruin.

After a few moments, Voss stopped pacing, breathing heavily. The silence in the room felt like a weight, pressing down on him, suffocating. He took one last look out the window at the city that had once felt like his playground, his empire, and saw it now for what it was—a fleeting place, a temporary realm, destined to crumble long before his legacy, whatever it would be, could take hold.

In his frustration, he considered calling Michael one last time, just to leave him with a parting shot, a reminder that he wouldn't be defeated so easily. But the idea felt hollow. What more could he say? He was a man grasping at straws, and Dominic would hear it in his voice, relish it, perhaps. No, he wouldn't give him the satisfaction.

With a bitter sigh, Voss moved away from the window, turning off the lights as he walked into the dim corridor leading to his bedroom. His plans had failed, his ambitions were in ruins, and he could already feel the painful sting of that realization settling into his bones. The bones that were his own—finite, flawed, and painfully human.

As he lay down, the darkness pressing in around him, Voss found himself face to face with the simple truth he had tried to escape. There would be no legacy, no immortal essence, no transcendence. He was just a man, and his days were numbered. And tonight, he was forced to accept that reality, however bitter it tasted.

CHAPTER

FORTY-FIVE

The late afternoon light filtered into Father Michael Dominic's Vatican office, casting soft, amber shadows over the stacks of books that covered every available surface. Hana Sinclair leaned forward, her elbows on Michael's desk, her face illuminated with the quiet thrill of discovery as she listened intently.

"So, let me get this straight," she said, her eyes alight with fascination. "You're saying Linus wasn't just some placeholder or name in the line of succession, but that he played a fundamental role in shaping what would become the Church, essentially building the Church along with Peter?"

Michael nodded, his gaze distant as he recalled the weight of Marcus Russo's recent findings. "Exactly. The inscriptions we've uncovered paint a picture of Linus as a pivotal figure—not just a custodian of Peter's teachings, but someone who saw the urgent need to carry on the work, adapting it for a community that was on the brink of fragmentation. It's like... it's like he was the bridge between the original followers and the formal structure of the early Church."

Hana's brow furrowed thoughtfully. "So he wasn't simply following in Peter's footsteps; he was making decisions about leadership, about who could conduct sacraments, and shaping the creeds? This was more than just preserving tradition—he was establishing it."

"Exactly," Michael said, a note of excitement entering his voice. "He understood that he had to act decisively, that the young faith could fracture without a strong foundation. Linus, in essence, was the one to both implement and expand on Peter's vision, refining and shaping it in ways we hadn't fully understood before now."

Hana's curiosity was clearly piqued. She leaned back, looking around the office as if searching for the right question among the rows of dusty volumes and loose notes. "Do you think there might be more records, more documents that give us a glimpse of this?"

A glint appeared in Michael's eye as he considered her question. "There may be," he said, almost to himself. "If Linus was as involved as these inscriptions suggest, there could very well be further references to him in our own manuscripts—possibly even documents that have gone unnoticed."

Without another word, he turned to his computer, tapping into the Vatican Archives' meticulous index of holdings. A few moments later, his eyes narrowed in concentration as he scrolled through pages of digitized records, looking for any entries that might correspond to Linus.

"Here," he said finally, tapping the screen. "References to Linus appear in a few manuscripts stored in the stacks. It's mostly catalogued as incidental mentions, but if there's anything that reinforces the role he played, those manuscripts could hold the answers."

Hana's face lit up with a mixture of excitement and anticipation. "We have to see them. Michael, this could be huge. I've never actually been in the stacks with you before—"

Michael raised an eyebrow, a hint of a smile playing at the corner of his mouth. "I'm not sure how much we'll find, but… I suppose there's only one way to know for certain." He leaned back, then extended his hand in invitation. "Are you ready to explore the archives?"

"Lead the way," Hana replied, trying—and failing—to hide her excitement.

Together, they made their way through the labyrinthine hallways of the Vatican, down narrow stairs, and through doorways hidden from public view, until they arrived at the entrance to the Vatican Archives. The air grew cooler as they descended deeper, the hum of distant generators and lights creating a faint, almost reverent silence. They passed through a final set of security checks before arriving at a heavy door leading into the restricted stacks.

Michael swiped his access card, and the door clicked open, revealing rows upon rows of ancient volumes and manuscripts housed in climate-controlled cases. Hana paused, taking in the sheer magnitude of the place.

Though she had been around the Vatican for years, she had never been granted access to the heart of the archives.

"It's even more amazing than I imagined," she murmured, her eyes wide as she took in the endless shelves, each filled with layers of history waiting to be uncovered.

Michael nodded, appreciating the awe in her voice. "It's something, isn't it? So much of the Church's history preserved in a single place. But come," he said, gesturing her forward. "We're looking for references to Linus. The catalog notes that they're stored in this section, but it may take a little time to find exactly what we're after."

They moved slowly down the aisle, Michael scanning the rows with a practiced eye. After a few minutes, he stopped, carefully pulling a thick manuscript bound in dark, cracked leather from the shelf.

"Ah, this should be one of them," he said, gently placing it on a nearby table and flipping open the cover with an almost reverent touch. "This manuscript appears to contain early Church records and letters— some of them attributed to the followers of Peter and Paul, those who knew them personally. Linus's name could be here, woven among the accounts."

Hana leaned over his shoulder, watching as he carefully turned the pages, the ancient parchment crinkling slightly under his touch. After a few minutes of reading in silence, Michael paused, his eyes fixed on a passage in faint Latin script.

"Here," he whispered, his finger tracing the lines. "A reference to Linus in a letter written by a follower of Paul, likely addressed to an early Christian leader in Rome. It describes Linus as him overseeing the formation of 'the creeds and rites in honor of the truth handed to him.'"

Hana exhaled, absorbing the significance of it all. "Michael, if he was creating rites and creeds, this wasn't a passive role. He was shaping the faith in a real, substantial way."

Michael nodded, feeling the weight of the discovery settle over him. "Linus was doing more than following. He was leading, laying the groundwork for a tradition that would endure through the centuries, shaping the very foundation of what we now consider doctrine. And yet... he remains one of history's more obscure figures."

Hana turned to him, her eyes filled with an almost reverent intensity. "He may have chosen to stay hidden, letting the legacy of Peter shine while he quietly ensured it would survive. There's something profound about that, isn't there? His humility—his willingness to serve without demanding recognition."

They sat in reflective silence, absorbing the resonance of Linus's hidden legacy. The dusty air felt charged with a sense of purpose, and in that moment, Michael felt a kinship with the man whose legacy they were uncovering—a quiet leader who had built a foundation not for glory, but for faith.

Finally, Michael broke the silence. "Hana, if we're truly going to understand Linus, there's more to be uncovered. I suspect he was involved in so much more than even these manuscripts can reveal. We might need to look through every record from that era to see where his influence left a mark."

Hana's face lit up with a mixture of awe and determination. "Then let's keep looking. I'm here to help, whatever it takes. If we're able to bring his story into the light, we'll be doing more than just understanding history. We'll be restoring a legacy."

They shared a quiet look, a mutual resolve passing between them. And as they turned back to the stacks, delving deeper into the Secret Archives, both knew they were setting off on a journey that might redefine not only the history of the Church but their own understanding of faith, legacy, and truth.

CHAPTER

FORTY-SIX

The archives were silent, the room heavy with the weight of history. Michael and Hana had been pouring over texts for hours, the only sound the faint rustling of ancient documents. As the evening light filtered through the high windows, casting a golden hue over the aged parchments, their proximity became increasingly charged with unspoken tension.

Michael looked up from a manuscript, his eyes meeting Hana's. The intensity of their shared gaze sent a shiver down his spine. He hadn't intended for this to happen, but the pull between them was undeniable. Without a word, he reached out, cupping her face gently with his hand. Hana's breath caught in her throat as he leaned in, his lips brushing softly against hers in a tentative kiss.

For a heartbeat, they paused, the world outside their small bubble forgotten. Then, as if something within them snapped, the kiss deepened, becoming more urgent and insistent. Hana folded her body into his, her hands clutching at the fabric of his shirt, feeling the warmth of his skin beneath. It felt as natural as breathing, as if they had always been meant to find each other in this moment.

Their kisses grew hungrier, a mix of passion and desperation. Michael's hands roamed over her back, pulling her closer, feeling the contours of her body against his. Hana responded in kind, her fingers tracing the line of his jaw, the curve of his neck. They moved together, a rhythm born out of need and a desire they could no longer deny.

They stumbled back, finding a small alcove where the shadows provided a semblance of privacy. Michael pressed his forehead against Hana's, his breath hitching as he felt the warmth of her body radiating through his. Through half-closed eyes, they watched each other, their lenses of perception blurred by insatiable longing. A faint tremor ran through Hana's fingers as they traced the outline of Michael's face, a map she had unknowingly committed to memory.

The grandeur around them dimmed as a world bloomed within the alcove—a world that belonged only to them—where every sigh was a proclamation of affection and every shared glance an affirmation of their illicit bond. The sinewy muscle beneath Hana's fingertips hardened with every stroke, eliciting soft gasps from Michael which echoed like sweet blasphemy in the hallowed corridors.

Their lips met again and again in fevered kisses, painting stories on each other's skin with a fervent urgency. Each pulse beat was a reminder of their fleeting time together; each stolen moment stitched them closer in an intricate tapestry of fervid passion and guilt.

The ancient walls bore silent witness to their union as they made tender love, a dance of guilt and pleasure intertwining with every touch, every whispered name. Each movement, each caress, was laced with an awkwardness that only intensified their connection. Neither could resist the magnetic pull of the other, despite the weight of their conscience pressing down on them.

In the throbbing silence of the Secret Archives, time ceased to exist. Each whisper of fabric against skin, each gasp of suppressed desire echoed in the vast, lonely space. The pale parchment papers, with their faded ink and age-old wisdom, seemed to sigh under the weight of their forbidden intimacy.

And when pleasure faded and reality seeped back into their senses, they found solace in silence. Their bodies lay intertwined amidst spectral shadows, words swallowed by the suffocating heaviness looming over them. The archives fell silent once more, holding its breath as if sharing their secret burden while the echoes of their passion slowly ebbed into oblivion, and the enormity of what had transpired began to sink in. They were both consumed by a mix of guilt and satisfaction, the knowledge that they had crossed a line they couldn't uncross lingering in the air between them. Yet neither spoke, for words would have shattered the fragile moment they had shared.

In the dim light, Michael brushed a stray lock of hair

from Hana's face, his touch lingering on her skin. Hana looked up at him, her eyes a blend of confusion and contentment. They knew that what had happened was forbidden, and yet, in that stolen moment, it had felt like the most natural thing in the world.

For a moment, neither of them moved, suspended in a fragile bubble where the world beyond the Vatican Archives didn't exist. But as the minutes ticked by, the gravity of what had transpired began to settle in. It wasn't just that they had made love—it was that this act had been building between them for so long, a current they could no longer ignore. The guilt was there, yes, an almost tangible presence between them. But so was something else. Something deeper. Something Michael could no longer pretend wasn't real.

His mind raced as he studied Hana's face, still flushed with the afterglow of their passion. He traced the curve of her jaw with his thumb, watching as her eyes fluttered shut for a moment, savoring his touch. This—this feeling—was something he hadn't expected, something he hadn't prepared for. He had always been careful, controlled, keeping his personal life separate from his duties. But now, with Hana, all those boundaries seemed to blur. He felt exposed, vulnerable in a way that both terrified and thrilled him.

He pulled her closer, inhaling the scent of her hair, feeling the steady rise and fall of her breath against his chest. There was something about being with her that quieted the noise in his head, the endless demands of his responsibilities. The Peter-Linus inscription, the exhibition of St. Peter's bones, the tightening grip of

Elliot Voss—all of it faded, if only for a moment, when he was with her. She grounded him, made him feel like more than just the Prefect of the Secret Archives, more than just a servant of the Church.

He had spent so much of his life devoted to his calling, to the mysteries and relics that shaped the faith of millions. But now, as he held Hana in his arms, he felt the stirrings of something he hadn't allowed himself to consider before. *What if there was more? What if he could have both?* The thought struck him with sudden clarity, his heart quickening as he considered the implications.

His mind flashed again to Pope Ignatius's dictum, the one that had upended centuries of tradition and allowed priests to marry. When it had been announced, Michael had thought of it only in abstract terms, as a theological shift that would affect others, not him. He had never seen himself as the type of priest who would consider marriage. His devotion had always been to the Church, and that had been enough.

Until Hana.

Now, the idea of marrying felt personal. He couldn't deny the pull he felt toward her, the way she had slowly become an anchor in his life. But even more than that, he couldn't deny the growing sense that his life as it was —filled with ancient manuscripts, diplomatic negotiations, and the weight of Church history—wasn't enough anymore. Not without her.

Michael exhaled slowly, his breath stirring a few strands of her hair. He knew Hana was as complicated as he was. Her life was full of danger, of stories that exposed the truth no matter the cost. She had her own burdens, her own risks. And yet, she was here, with him, in this moment, and the connection between them felt undeniable.

But was he ready for what came next? Was she?

He had to know.

"Hana," he said softly, his voice barely a whisper in the quiet room. She stirred in his arms, lifting her gaze to meet his, her eyes still hazy from their shared moment. "I've been thinking…"

Her brows furrowed slightly, curiosity flickering across her face. "About what?" she asked, her voice equally soft, as if the air between them was too fragile for anything louder.

Michael hesitated, searching for the right words. This wasn't just about the physical connection they had shared; it was about something far deeper. Something that had been growing between them for months, perhaps even longer. He couldn't imagine his life without her in it, couldn't imagine facing the mounting pressures of his work without her support, her presence.

"I miss you," he admitted, the words spilling out before he could stop them. "I miss us—having more time together. I know our lives are complicated. The things we're both dealing with… they're overwhelming." His voice dropped lower. "But I need more of you in my life. I can't keep compartmentalizing, pretending that I don't… want you, that I don't need you. Not anymore."

Hana blinked, her expression softening, though a trace of hesitation lingered in her eyes. She reached up, brushing her fingers gently along his jaw, her touch calming him even as his heart raced. "Michael... I feel the same. But... we live in different worlds. How would this even work?" Her voice was tentative, laced with uncertainty.

Michael swallowed hard, his thoughts spinning as he prepared to voice the words that had been weighing on his heart. She was right—they did live in different worlds. But if his years in the archives had taught him anything, it was that the most meaningful connections often defied logic, transcending the barriers between time, space, and circumstance. Love, like the relics he so carefully preserved, was eternal in its essence.

"I don't have all the answers," he said, his voice steady but filled with emotion. "But I know this: I'm tired of living with half my heart in one world and half in another. I want us to be together—not just in these fleeting moments, but always."

Hana's eyes softened, her expression a blend of surprise and curiosity.

Michael hesitated only a beat, his nerves giving way to a flicker of boldness. A faint, mischievous smile curved his lips. "You know... there is one simple solution to this dilemma."

Her brow arched slightly, her intrigue evident. "Oh? And what might that be?"

He tightened his hold on her hand, his gaze locked on hers. The words caught briefly in his throat before spilling out with surprising clarity. "Marry me, Hana."

The air between them stilled, heavy with the weight of his unexpected proposal. He watched her, her lips parting in astonishment as she blinked, trying to process what she had just heard. It wasn't planned—it wasn't polished. But it was true, and in that moment, nothing else mattered.

After a beat, Hana's lips curved into a radiant, teasing smile, her eyes glimmering with warmth and delight. "Well, Michael," she said softly, her voice tinged with affectionate humor, "it certainly took you long enough."

Michael let out a breath he hadn't realized he was holding, a chuckle breaking through his tension. "I wanted to get it right," he said, his grin widening. "And I wasn't about to rush something this important."

Her laughter bubbled up, light and joyful, before her expression turned serious, though no less tender. "You're sure about this? About us?"

"I've never been more certain of anything," he replied, his voice firm but gentle. "This isn't about solving a problem or making a compromise. It's about choosing you. Every day, every moment. Whatever comes, we'll face it together."

Hana nodded, her smile unwavering. "Then yes. Of course, yes."

Relief flooded through him as he pulled her into his arms, their worlds finally aligning in a way that felt both impossible and inevitable. In that moment, it didn't matter where they came from or what challenges lay ahead. What mattered was this—their love, a steadfast compass pointing them toward a shared future they were ready to embrace.

EPILOGUE

Father Michael Dominic knelt in the small, faintly lit chapel within Domus Santa Marta, his hands clasped tightly together in prayer. The familiar scent of incense lingered in the air, rising like the silent prayers of centuries of clergy before him. The flickering light of the votive candles danced across the altar, leaving shadows over the ancient icons and statues that had borne witness to countless supplications and confessions.

But tonight, it was his heart that was heavy. It was his soul that sought answers.

In front of him lay the decision that had consumed his thoughts for days—ever since Hana had said yes. Ever since he had asked her to be his wife. The joy of that moment still filled him, even now, but beneath it was the growing weight of the choice that followed. The one he had known would come but hadn't wanted to face.

Could he be a priest *and* a husband? Could he divide his heart between two callings without diminishing either?

His entire life had been devoted to the Church. From the moment he had entered the seminary, his path had seemed clear. The priesthood had been his anchor, his way of serving God, of finding purpose. And for years, it had been enough. He had poured his heart and soul into his vocation, into his work with the Apostolic Archives, guarding the Church's secrets, preserving its history. His devotion had been total. And yet…

Hana had changed everything.

Michael took a deep breath, his thoughts swirling like the clouds of incense that rose before the altar. He had never expected to fall in love, not in the way that he had with Hana. What had begun as mutual respect, shared intellectual pursuits, and an undeniable chemistry had grown into something much deeper—something neither of them could ignore. The joy he felt when he was with her, the peace she brought to his restless mind, the way she saw him not just as a priest but as *Michael*, the man—it was more than he had ever thought he could have.

But now, with their engagement, the reality of what it meant weighed on him more than ever. He had prayed for guidance, sought answers in scripture and in the quiet of his own heart, but the clarity he had hoped for hadn't come easily.

The truth was, he couldn't have both—not fully. Marriage wasn't just a ceremony or a promise exchanged in a church. It was a life—a shared life. It required presence, commitment, time. It demanded his energy, his devotion, in ways that being a Jesuit priest wouldn't allow. The vows he had made as a priest had shaped him for so long that stepping away from them felt like tearing away a piece of his soul. And yet, how could he offer Hana anything less than all of himself?

He shifted on the pew, his gaze drifting up to the large crucifix above the altar. In that moment, he felt the full weight of the cross he now carried—the tension between his love for Hana and his love for the Church. His heart ached with the struggle. But even as the conflict waged within him, something was slowly coming into focus.

He had known, deep down, what the answer was. From the moment he had proposed to Hana, he had known that the life he had led as a Jesuit priest wasn't one he could continue if he wanted to fully honor his commitment to her. He had been trying to hold onto both worlds, but it was becoming clear that he couldn't. Not in the way either deserved.

To be *fully married* to Hana—to be the husband she deserved—he would need to be present in a way that his priestly duties wouldn't allow. The late nights, the constant demands of the Church, the regular Masses, the responsibility of his role as Prefect of the Apostolic Archives—it all required a kind of singular focus. He had seen it before in other clergy who had married under the new guidelines. They had struggled, torn between their families and the Church. Some managed, but many didn't. And Michael couldn't risk that—not with Hana.

His thoughts turned to her now, to the way she had looked at him when he proposed, the way she had smiled, her eyes full of hope and love. She deserved more than a part-time husband, someone constantly pulled away by the duties of the Church. She deserved his full heart, his full attention.

Michael's breath hitched in his throat as the realization settled deep within him: *he would have to leave the priesthood.*

The decision, though painful, felt strangely right. He knew what it would cost him—the community, the sense of purpose, the life of service that had defined him. But it would also give him something he had never allowed himself to fully dream of—a life with Hana. A future. A family, perhaps.

Michael's thoughts turned to St. Linus, the humble successor to St. Peter, who served the Church not through grandeur or acclaim, but through quiet dedication to its mission. Linus had carried the weight of leadership without fanfare, his name barely whispered in the annals of history, yet his contributions were profound, his service unwavering. Michael realized, with a clarity that both comforted and challenged him, that his own life might take on a similar shape.

Like Linus, he could still serve the Church, not bound by titles or vestments, but through the integrity of his faith and the steadfastness of his actions. The priesthood had given him structure and purpose, but it wasn't the sole conduit of his devotion. His path would shift, but his commitment to God, to truth, and to helping others would remain his compass.

He saw his life as a mosaic, much like the ones that adorned the Vatican—its pieces varied and imperfect, but together forming a design greater than any single fragment. Stepping away from the priesthood wouldn't shatter his identity; it would simply rearrange the tiles, allowing new colors and patterns to emerge. With Hana by his side, their life together could become an extension of his service, rooted in love and guided by faith.

He may not stand at the altar as a priest again, but his soul would still kneel in reverence before God. He would carry the spirit of Linus within him—quiet, faithful, and resolute, serving the Church and its people not from the pulpit, but from the sacred space of his heart.

He rose slowly from his knees, his legs stiff from the long hours of prayer. As he stood before the altar, he made the sign of the cross, feeling the familiar motions steady him, even in this moment of upheaval. He wasn't abandoning God—he would never do that. His faith was still growing, his love for the Church unshaken. But he knew that his path was diverging from the one he had once thought was his only calling.

And yet... there was one part of his work he couldn't bear to give up: the Apostolic Archives. The Vatican's vast repository of history, the secrets of the Church he had dedicated years of his life to protecting and preserving. It wasn't just a job; it was a passion, a calling in its own right. Leaving the priesthood didn't have to mean abandoning the archives. He could serve the Church in other ways—ways that didn't require him to remain bound by the vows of the Jesuit order.

As he turned and walked slowly down the aisle, his footsteps echoing in the empty chapel, he began to formulate a plan. He would approach his superiors, explain his decision. He would push to remain in his position as Prefect of the Apostolic Archives, to continue the work that had been his life's mission. His priesthood might end, but his connection to the Church did not have to. He could still serve, still protect the history that mattered so much to him. It would be a difficult conversation, no doubt. But he had to try.

Michael stepped out into the cool night air, the stillness of the Vatican grounds surrounding him like a quiet benediction. For the first time in days, he felt a sense of peace settle over him. The path ahead wouldn't be easy, and the sacrifices would be great. But as he thought of Hana—her smile, her laughter, the way she made him feel alive—he knew that he was making the right choice.

He would leave the priesthood, but he wouldn't leave his faith. And with Hana by his side, he would find a new way forward—a new life, built on love, on partnership, on the promise of something deeper than the confines of any one calling.

With that, he made his way back to his apartment in Domus Santa Marta, his heart lighter, his mind clearer. Tomorrow, he would begin the process of stepping away from the priesthood. But tonight, he would hold onto the knowledge that for the first time in a long time, he had chosen a path not only for his faith, but for his future. For their future.

~

FICTION, FACT, OR FUSION

Many readers have asked me to distinguish fact from fiction in my books. Generally, I like to take factual events and historical figures and build on them creatively—but much of what I do write is historically accurate. In this book, I'll review some of the chapters where questions may arise, with hopes it might help those wondering where reality meets creative writing.

PROLOGUE:

Every word of the Prologue is true, based on historical references, biblical passages, and oral traditions.

CHAPTERS 10+15:

St. Linus was, in fact, the successor to St. Peter, traditionally the first two popes of the Roman Catholic Church (long before the Church was officially organized). There is no argument as to who was first and who was second; the "equal" standing created here is fictional.

CHAPTER 46:

Finally, at long last, Michael and Hana consummated their relationship, taking it to the next level. I really struggled with this chapter. The choice to have Michael and Hana make love in the Secret Archives is deeply symbolic and emotionally charged, reflecting the culmination of years of suppressed longing, unspoken connection, and mutual respect. The setting—steeped in history and secrecy—mirrors the intimacy and vulnerability of their act, a moment where duty and discipline give way to raw, undeniable human emotion. Yes, it was impulsive and bypassed traditional courtship, but the intensity of their shared experiences and the trust they've built over time made this moment feel both inevitable and natural. It is less about sin or convention and more about two people finally surrendering to the depth of their bond, a collision of passion and timing that defies easy categorization or judgment.

EPILOGUE:

Logically, Michael wrestles with whether or not he should remain in the priesthood. Frankly, I haven't made a decision on this one way or another going forward, though I believe I've made a strong case for him leaving. On the other hand, remaining in the priesthood will present challenges that are too attractive for a writer to ignore. So this is just a heads-up to stay tuned…

~

AUTHOR'S NOTE

Dealing with issues of theology, religious beliefs, and the fictional treatment of historical biblical events can be a daunting affair.

I would ask all readers to view this story for what it is—a work of pure fiction, adapted from the seeds of many oral traditions and the historical record, at least as we know it today.

Apart from telling an engaging story, I have no agenda here, and respect those of all beliefs, from Agnosticism to Zoroastrianism and everything in between.

Thank you for reading *The Apostle Conspiracy*. I hope you enjoyed it and, if you haven't already, suggest you pick up the story in the earlier books of The Magdalene Chronicles series—*The Magdalene Deception, The Magdalene Reliquary,* and *The Magdalene Veil*—and look forward to forthcoming books featuring the same characters and a few new ones in the continuing *Vatican Secret Archive Thrillers* series.

When you have a moment, **may I ask that you leave a review on Amazon**, Goodreads, Facebook and perhaps elsewhere you find convenient? Reviews are crucial to a book's success, and I hope for The Magdalene Chronicles and the Vatican Secret Archive Thrillers series to have a long and entertaining life.

You can easily leave your review by going to my Amazon book page for *The Apostle Conspiracy*. And thank you!

If you would like to reach out for any reason, you can email me at gary@garymcavoy.com. If you'd like to learn more about me and my other books, visit my website at www.garymcavoy.com, where you can also sign up for my private mailing list.

With kind regards,

Gary McAvoy

Made in United States
Troutdale, OR
12/12/2024

26341744R10178